HAYDEN

A FOUR SONS STORY

Amy ♡

Pearson's Rule!

J.D. HOLLYFIELD

Hayden

Copyright © 2018 J.D. Hollyfiel

Cover Design: All By Design
Photo: Adobe Stock
Editor: Wordnerd Editing
Formatting: Raven Designs

I am a hothead, a wild card, and son to a murdered man.
I crave the things I can't have and don't want the things I can.

Now, I'm left to pick up the pieces—stitch our family back
together with a damaged thread.
This isn't the life I envisioned. And to make matters worse,
the women in our lives are testing the strength of our
brotherhood.

My name is Hayden Pearson.

I am the eldest—a protective, but vindictive son.
People may think I'm too young to fill our father's shoes, but
it won't stop me from proving them all wrong.

DEDICATION

This one goes out to all my readers.

I would be nowhere without your love for filthy books.

Keep on keepin' on.

My father isn't dead.

I'm staring right at him.

ONE

H A Y D E N

S ELFISH. SPOILED. UNAPOLOGETIC.

That's who's staring back at me. A constant reminder of the person I am. Who I've become. A man who sees something he wants and takes it.

Just like him.

A set of familiar steel blue eyes stare back through the reflection in the full-length mirror.

Just like his.

Fresh out of the shower, I stand in front of the mirror inspecting myself. I follow the droplets of water as they drip from my wet hair and down my face. My hair is overgrown and in need of a cut. The scowl I constantly wear is just another indication.

I am no different than him.

No, I am *exactly* like him.

The steaming hot water after a long run does nothing to thaw out the ice in my Pearson veins. I rake my hands through my wild hair and watch as more water slides down my lean chest. Not an ounce of fat hides behind my tan physique. Another Pearson gene. One I can appreciate. Unlike the rest of the vindictive traits he passed down.

My father has been rotting six feet under for the last two years, but the essence of his darkness is still very much alive. It lives and breathes inside me. The need to control and conquer. To own and destroy. My father didn't raise his four sons with the vision of us blossoming into decent, honorable men. No, he made sure we were groomed to become leaders. Fearless warriors. Emotion was not a quality important to Eric Pearson. He used to always say emotions made a person weak. Vulnerable to one's enemies. And he was right. Because that's who I'm surrounded by.

I pull the towel from my waist and toss it to the floor. Stepping into my briefs, I adjust my cock comfortably and head into my large walk-in closet to dress for work. Four Fathers Freight, a company I now run. I have three other partners, but I'm the one holding all the cards. My father made sure of that.

Sometimes, I wonder if he knew he was going to die. The plan he left in his will sure as fuck made it feel that way. But he also knew he raised a leader. And that's why he left it all to me. The house, the company, responsibility of my three brothers—all the burdens he carried now lie on my shoulders.

Another reason for me to hate my father.

I didn't want this. I wanted out. But my father decided to get his head blown off for underage pussy and now I'm leading the pack.

Fuck you, Dad. Fuck you.

But as the infamous Eric Pearson would say: "*I always get what I want. In business. In life. In the sack. Always.*"

—————

The sound of the television blaring from the living room as I walk through the condo Camden and I moved into three months ago tells me my brother is already awake. Knowing him, he's been up for hours watching CNN or another political debate channel he's been obsessed with. I'm pretty sure his first words were "foreign trade." I always tell him he's too pretty to be in politics, but the truth is, Cam is a triple threat: wealth, brains, looks—and he's not even eighteen yet. He's going to run the world one day, I'm sure of it. A force to be reckoned with.

"You ever sleep?" I ask, turning the corner to enter the lavish, state-of-the-art, marble kitchen and opening the fridge for a drink. I don't know how I stayed in our family home so long after our lives changed. Two years ago, we buried our father. We mourned the loss of a man all four of us loved but hated just the same. Right after it happened, I fought the urge to burn the whole place down. I wanted to rid us all of the fucked-up memories that house held. But I quickly learned you can't rid yourself of scars. You don't erase the memory of your father getting shot and killed by a psychopath in front of you or the realization of where your mother had been all these years.

In the beginning, I tried keeping us all together. But shit just kept getting fucked up. Eventually, Nixon and Ro took off. Brock was into his own fucked up shit. He left shortly after for college and barely came home. Cam was still a minor, which fell on me as his legal guardian. That's right. Overnight, I went from the wild, no-fucks kid to a parent to my youngest brother. Not to mention, CEO to a multi-billion-dollar freight company. All because my father couldn't keep his old ass dick in his pants and away from Ro—the one who should have been anyone's but his.

But finally, I was done. Living too close to the memories was doing more harm than good.

"I can ask you the same thing," Cam chimes back. "You were already gone when I woke up at four."

Shit, I must have slept in. I'm normally up and out the door by three, needing the quietness of the world around me while I run. I've always been athletic. It's in our Pearson genes. But as of late, or should I say the last two years, I've been pushing myself, running 'til my muscles burn and my lungs give out to help myself stay focused. I need it to stay focused.

Some days, I think Jax Wheeler did us all a favor. He got rid of the one person who was supposed to show us love. Teach us how to be good men. But instead, he only taught us how to be cold and heartless. I hated my father for what he created in us all. And when Jax took his life, the mess he left for me...it only made me resent him more.

My father never discussed what would happen with Four Fathers if anything ever happened to him. I'm sure he never expected to be offed for his inappropriate behavior. The way he looked at her—treated her—I would be lying if I said the same murderous thoughts as her father hadn't run through my brain. Who knows. Maybe if Wheeler didn't take out my father, it would have eventually been one of his own sons.

"You gotta work all day?" Camden asks, turning off the TV and joining me in the kitchen.

"Yeah. Partners' staff meeting." Which makes me want to put a fist through the wall. For the past two years, I've been busting my ass trying to prove myself to those assholes. And all I get in return is anger and resentment, like I stole something from them. My father's will didn't leave his shares to his partners. Not even his best friend. He left them to me. His first born. The news shocked everyone, including me. I had no interest in touching Four Fathers. I couldn't give a fuck what happened to it. To be honest, I just wanted whatever insurance money dear old dad left for each of us and take off. But even six feet under, my father is still fucking with my life. He didn't just leave me his shares, he made sure I couldn't turn around and sell them. I guess maybe he did know me better than I'd thought.

The stipulations in his will were as stated: I was to inherit his fifty-one percent in the company. Yeah. That's right. That meant I was the primary shareholder of Four Fathers. But there were terms involved. Bold writing that stated I was not to sell off my shares until I was twenty-five. He made sure I had no choice but to stick it out and run his company. At that point, if I still wanted to sell, I was to sell my shares to the one person my father saw as family: Trevor Blackstone.

"You think Uncle Trev is gonna get on you again?"

I grab a power drink from the fridge and slam the door shut. "He's not our uncle. Stop fucking calling him that. And if he tries, I'll put his ass in his place like I always do."

"You know he's only trying to help you though, right? Dad would have wanted us to lean on him if we ever needed—"

"We don't fucking need him. God, wake up, Cam. He's not family. He's no one to us. He was Dad's best friend. And Dad's gone. He just wants my shares and is kissing my ass like a fucking weasel until I'm twenty-five." Little does he know, he's not getting shit. I may act like I want nothing to do with Four Fathers, but you don't give someone this much power then hand it away. All the time I've invested, it's mine—and that's how it's staying.

I lean against the marble counter and take a swig of my drink as I stare out the window. The view is impeccable. You don't get a view like this without paying a small fortune. The condo looks over downtown Tampa all the way to the bluest waters of the ocean. Cam comes to stand in front of me and folds his arms, making the muscles tense. Little shit is nearly as built as me now. Guess we both use working out as a release.

"Speaking of time, you know what's next week, right?"

My fingers tighten around the bottle. The crunch of

the plastic sounds as my knuckles turn white. Next week will officially be two years. The anniversary of his death. "I know what fucking next week is." I guzzle the rest of my drink and toss the empty bottle into the garbage. I turn to Cam, who looks sullen. My mood swiftly changes, and guilt settles in. I may have hated my father, but Cam didn't. He misses him. He still talks about him as if he were this great man. Great father. He was just too young to understand what kind of man Eric Pearson really was.

It doesn't help that the same day he lost his father, he learned where his whore of a mother had been the past eight years. That shock hit us all more than watching our father die before our eyes. Eight years, we all convinced ourselves she didn't love us and left. We weren't good enough for her. And she'd been dead the whole time. Mere fucking yards from our home.

"Well, I just wanted to remind you since I know you've had a lot on your plate lately. I reached out to Nixon, but he hasn't returned my text. Same with Brock.

I thought he would be home for summer break already. You don't think they'd forget, do you?"

Who would want to remember? Even if they tried, no one could scrape away the fucked-up scenario we all witnessed. Rowan, Dad—Wheeler shooting both. The skeletal remains of our mother floating up in the heavy rain. Time doesn't seem to make the memory any more distant. And every year when we have to relive it, it sets us all on edge.

"They won't forget. Stop worrying about it. Focus on school. Get the fuck out of here like you've always planned." I head back to my room, stopping next to him, and rest my palm on his shoulder. The small but quick endearment lets him know I've got his back. I didn't ask to be where I am, but god knows I won't let my brother get dragged down because of our father's mess.

I head out and jump into my Bugatti Chiron, bringing her to a quick purr. The condo is a quick ride through the city to the office, which is how I like it. In a short time, I pull into the private underground parking of Four Fathers Freight. The strange feeling never goes away. The intense sensation inside my gut reminding me I hold all the power. There might be three other partners, but as the years pass, I get a better understanding of how powerful my father truly was. Because that power lies in my hands. Nothing in this company happens unless I say it happens. I make the final decisions and call all the shots.

Since the moment I slipped right into my father's seat, I've been baited, propositioned, and sweet talked into selling off my shares. Levi was the worst. That asshole was the first one banging down my door. Offering a trade in pussy. Telling me I could have it all, and he'd show me the way, just sign over a few to him and my life would be set with the tightest cunts alive. Little did that asshole know, I got more pussy than his old ass ever did. Plus, seems his playing cards have been long revoked since he's married with a kid on the way. Really killed his game.

Lately, all he does is brag about his monthly blow jobs from his cranky ass wife.

Mateo never pushed. He may have thrown a few hints that he was interested if I was offering, but other than that, he's been cool to me. Never tried too hard to convince me to sell. He spent more time offering advice on running the business. I respected him for that.

But Trevor, I couldn't be in a room longer than five minutes without wanting to pummel his face in. He was supposed to be my dad's best friend—the only guy my father trusted. I don't even think he trusted his own children. Shit, he even *loved* Trevor more than us. When Nixon suggested Trevor was his dad, I'd set the record straight. I'd seen the files our father had in his will, and the paternity results all came back clear: we were Eric Pearson's sons—Nixon included.

Much to Nixon's, and if I were being honest, my surprise.

Trevor even looked relieved that day at the hospital.

Because you'd have to be blind not to see the similarities in their features, and Nixon has the same obsessive personality as Trevor. If I hadn't seen the results myself, I would've questioned it too. I was content knowing he wasn't—until that fucking night, four months ago I learned Trevor was a lying cunt. Turns out, he did fuck my whore mother. I knew it. And now I needed to expose him for the lying piece of shit he is.

Four months ago...

I'm pushing through a bunch of boxes that have been stored in the attic for too many years to even remember. I don't even know why I'm up here. This isn't the first time I drank myself into a stupor and came up here, tearing the place apart. Why? I have no fucking idea. I know when we get rid of this place, we'll have to do something with all this shit. I see boxes with my and my brothers' names on them. Baby clothes. Toys. Kids bedding. Too bad there's not one labeled weed and pills. I could really use them to chase this drunken high like nobody's business.

I kick a box, knocking over some old shirts, when I come across a wooden chest. It has a lock with no key and the letters JB, my mother's initials before she was married carved into the wood.

I'm confused as to why my father kept it. He'd tossed, burned, cut...shit, he did everything in his power to get rid of everything that reminded him of her.

It's the only thing I've come across up here that's been hers.

Rubbing my hand over the soft wood, I debate whether or not to open it. Curiosity gets the better of me and I dig through a toolbox for some bolt cutters.

A few of my mother's personal things lay inside. Her birth certificate, some old letters my dad wrote to her. A few baby pictures of us kids. I dig further to find a small hand gun. I'm tempted to take it and go back to the pool and shoot Brock in the ass with it.

Ever since Dad died, he thinks he can do whatever the fuck he wants.

I push it to the side, and dig even further, until something catches my eye. A letter. It's not from my dad, but the handwriting is familiar. I pull it from the envelope, and a picture falls out from nestled inside. Is that Trevor? Why would Mom have a photo of Trevor in her box? He must be in his early twenties. The photograph is old. From the wear and tear, it's been crumpled and re-flattened more than a dozen times. It's hard to truly make out the face, but it looks similar to Trevor. I flip the photo over and read the handwritten name on the back—in Trevor's script. Jameson Vincent. Who the fuck is Jameson Vincent? I take another hard look at the man, and the certainty inside my gut starts piecing it together. His build, hair color...it's got to be Trevor. Was Trevor an old flame of my mom's before she met my dad?

I open up the letter, and my gut drops.

Trevor, you have to make this go away for me. You promised.

The words in black pen are scribbled in my mother's writing over a DNA test—a replica of the ones in our father's will. This is Nixon's, and the results say he's not a match to Eric. What the fuck?

Turning over the paper, I find a post-it note stuck to it.

He can never know it was me!

Motherfucker! That's Trevor's writing again. So, he is Nixon's father? Who the hell is Jameson? An alias?

My hands begin to shake as the anger rolls in. All these years. He's been acting like a father figure to Nixon, and now it makes sense why. My mother's been gone for years, but I still remember the way she looked at him—flirted with him.

I crumple the photo in my hands.

The urge to find Trevor and punch him 'til he's begging for his life boils inside me. I take the photo and flip it over again.

Jameson Vincent.

Why would he change his name?

I remember the stories of him being homeless. His life struggles going through homes, until he met my father at college. Did my father even know if Trevor Blackstone was his real name?

Thoughts and conspiracies begin spinning inside my fucked-up head. Is Trevor Vincent? Did my mother know him before my father? Had they been having an affair the whole time?

He is not getting away with this. He may have fooled my entire family, but he's not going to fool me. I stuff the photo in my back pocket and pull out my phone. Scrolling through my contacts, I reach the name I'm looking for and press call.

"Evans..."

"Chip, it's Hayden Pearson."

"Oh, s'up, Hayden? Sorry to hear about your old man. Fucked up shit, man."

Only fucked up thing is it didn't happen years ago. "Yeah. I need your help. I need that contact of the private investigator you said you knew. The one who would dig in the dirtiest holes to get the job done..."

It's been four months, and nothing. Brandon Wyatt, my private investigator proved a Trevor Blackstone existed in the hospital records, but it did nothing to ease my suspicions. Anyone could obtain that shit nowadays. The deep, dark web is an amazing resource when you need something illegal.

It took this asshole almost a month to get Jameson Vincent on his radar. A man, fitting the description, was living down in Alabama, but the age was off by twelve years. One after another, dead ends, fake addresses, and phony information. All clues telling me Trevor wasn't who he said he was. He was just one step ahead of me every time.

But not today.

Today, I got a call from my guy. He found him. And for a bonus fee, he would give me the answers I've spent the last four months obsessing over. Once I get done with this goddamn partner meeting, I'm closing in on Trevor. He has no idea what's coming for him. He won't even see the destruction before I ruin him.

TWO

H A Y D E N

"**S**o, I let her suck me off with her sexy as fuck mouth until I made a mess of her face. I swear, my girl knows how to take me down with those sweet lips."

I hear Mateo laugh at Levi's pathetic comment about his wife. She probably chokes on his dirty ass cock every time.

Everyone's chair turns toward the door as I enter the large conference room of Four Fathers. "Oh, wow, the golden child graces us with his presence," Levi says, trying to bait me as I walk past him. I don't waste my time feeding into his jabs and allow my middle finger to do the talking for me. I sit at the head of the table, just as my father would have, and throw my legs atop. "Morning,

gentleman. Sorry to keep you waiting. Actually...I'm not."
I don't give a shit if they have to wait for me. I turn to
Trevor, who has that tick to him. He's about to tell me
just how late I am in nanoseconds.

I toss the folder with this quarter's latest numbers
and prospective clients and watch as it slides down the
table, stopping in front of Mateo. "Here's the list of this
quarter's numbers. They're up twenty-seven percent
from last quarter. The lead I followed, getting all those
mom and pop shipping companies in Cleveland, was a
success. A little convincing and a few threats. You're all
welcome for that." I may have been thrown into this role,
but the moment I sat down in my father's pristine leather
chair, I made sure to own the title I inherited. Because
fuck up or not, I wasn't going to let them prove I couldn't
handle the pressure. My father may have taken the choice
away from me, but now that I was in it, I was going to
dominate it. Two years later, and the company is doing
even better than when my father was alive.

"As always, good job, Hayden," Mateo says, picking up the file to flip through the documents. "I thought some of the Cleveland based companies refused to sell?"

"Money talks. With a little convincing, they folded like a cheap suit."

Tapping comes from the far end of the table where Trevor sits. It puts a smile on my face knowing just how much he disapproves of my ways. Well, like father, like son, he will continue to deal with it.

"Anywho, that settles this meeting. 'Til next time, you fossils." Laughing, I swing my legs off the table and stand. Mateo always allows my insults to roll off him, unlike Levi, who takes great offense in being called old, even though he is.

"Call me a fossil again, kid. I'm not too old to kick your ass."

"I dare you to try, old man," I threaten, then walk out. This is how it's been for the last two years. No one can deny I've made this company billions.

In the last two years, Four Fathers went from the third largest to second largest transport operating company in the US, and the net-worth has increased by two billion. I may have had my dick deep in every hot female professor I had, but the short time I was at college, I paid attention. I knew business like the back of my hand. My father not only did us four sons a favor by getting his head blown off, but his partners for allowing me to take control.

I head back toward the receptionist so I can flirt with the hot little blonde before I have to meet my guy.

"Hayden, wait."

I cringe at the sound of Trevor's voice. I stop only because this may be the last time I see him at Four Fathers. Once I get the information I need, he'll be done here.

I turn to face him. "What can I do for you, Trevor?"

"Just wanted to see how you're doing, son."

"Don't fucking call me son. I'm *not* your son." I watch him instantly back off. Time and time again, he insists to coddle me, as if he cares about me and my family. No man sleeps with their best friend's wife, conceives a child, and calls themselves a loyal friend.

"Understood. I just wanted to reach out to see how you're doing. I know next week is the anniversary. I wanted to know if you—"

"I need nothing from you, man. When are you going to get that through your head?"

"Never. You can act like a tough fuckin' prick all you want, but for your father, I won't ever stop looking after you four. He was my family too."

"Oh, give me a fucking break. Really? You're going to pull this shit with me again? Why don't you just drop the fucking act? You didn't care about my dad."

Trevor's brows crinkle. I know that statement always hits home with him. I know they went through a lot when they were together at college. How my dad saved him. "You have no idea what your father meant to me."

At that, I let out a cynical laugh. "Give me a break, old man. You may have everyone else fooled, but you aren't fooling me. And soon, everyone will know the truth."

"What truth is that, *son*?"

That motherfucker. Baiting me is not in his best interest.

"You mean Nixon? 'Cause you and I both know who your *real* son is. Better get your affairs in order. Your perfect little life is about to go boom."

Trevor's eyes widen. I've caught him off guard. *Damn right I know the truth, asshole.* He takes a dominating step toward me when his phone rings that familiar tone. Lucy. He wouldn't dare let her call go to voicemail. He pauses, and I watch him begin to count. He gets to five, takes a step back, and pulls his phone from his suit pocket.

"Baby, everything okay?" he answers, never taking his eyes off me. "When? I thought she got in tomorrow? Okay. No, my meeting is done. I'll pick her up. Tell Katie to look for me instead of you. Okay. Love you too."

Katie.

Katie.

Katie.

FUCK.

The name dissipates any anger I feel toward Trevor.

Katie.

Katie.

My Katie.

"I don't know what the fuck you're up to, but you're wrong. And we're not done here," he says before storming past me. Once he gets to the elevator and the door opens, he steps in and turns to lock eyes with me. "And don't even fucking think about it." And the doors shut.

———

A year and a half ago...

I've been sitting in the waiting room for over six hours. Beside me is Camden, who's somehow managed to fall asleep even with everything going on. Nixon hasn't returned, and I have no idea what the fuck is going on. He begged me to stay and protect Rowan, but I don't even know from what. Shortly after Nixon took off, an ambulance brought in an unconscious Lucy. I haven't seen Trevor since they brought her in, but he didn't look good at all.

I get up again and check to see if the nurse can give me any information on Lucy. Of course, the cunt won't, since I'm not family. Trevor hasn't come back to the waiting room, so we have no idea what's happening. The nurse kicked Cam and I out of Rowan's room a couple hours ago because visiting hours were over. Even after I threatened her, almost getting thrown out of the hospital, and Cam working his charm, she still wouldn't let us stay. I've had my eyes peeled to the entrance for any red flags.

The doors open, and a female comes running to the front desk. Her hair is disheveled, her eyes swollen. I assume she's been crying.

"My best friend. She was brought in here hours ago. S— She...I need to see her. Now!"

The girl becomes hysterical, banging her palms on the counter, demanding a room number. The nurse doesn't look happy.

"I'm her best friend! That is family! Lucy Marshall, what fucking room is she in, bitch!"

Lucy.

I move Cam's head off my shoulder and move toward the reception desk.

"Miss, if you don't calm down, I'm gonna have to call—"

"Bitch, you're gonna have to call security to rip me off you if you don't tell me what room she's—"

"Lucy? Trevor Blackstone's Lucy?" I say, and she

whips around, peering up at me. Her emerald eyes are filled with tears, and her cheeks are stained with wetness. Her lips are also swollen. I imagine from her chewing on them.

"Yes! Do you know her? Are you Trevor's son? Is she okay? Can you take me to her?" Question after question, she spits out. The nurse has the receiver in her hand, ready and waiting to see the girl's next move.

"Yes, I know her. I'm Hayden Pearson. My dad is—or was, Trevor's best friend."

She seems to calm some, taking me in. "Yes, yes, I've heard of you. Can you please take me to Lucy? Trevor said she wasn't conscious. It didn't look good. Oh god, is she still alive? They wouldn't give me any updates on the phone and this bitch won't even tell me her room number."

She starts to cry.

Grabbing her, I pull her into my embrace and walk her over to where Cam is still fast asleep. "Here, just take a seat. They won't let you in since you're not family. That's why we're all out here."

She looks around, her eyes landing on Cam.

"That's my brother, Camden. Here, sit. They won't tell you anything, no matter how upset you get. Trust me, I was in your shoes a couple hours ago."

She debates it a few seconds before giving in and falling into the chair. I sit next to her, and we're both quiet as we stare at the hospital doors, waiting for them to swing open. An hour goes by and still no word. Her hands are restless, so I reach out and thread my fingers through hers. It's strange, since she's a complete stranger, but it feels right comforting her. She looks at me and nods, offering me a silent thanks, and brings her eyes back to the door.

I find myself brushing my thumb along the top of her hand. Her skin is smooth and pale, telling me she doesn't live anywhere with constant sun like Tampa. There's a sweet scent in the air, one that wasn't here before her.

I want to lift her hand and smell her skin. Maybe take my tongue and taste her. Just as my mind goes dark wondering what she smells like down below, the doors burst open and Trevor runs through them. His eyes are bloodshot and frantic as he searches the waiting room. He spots me, then the girl next to me.

"Katie," he calls, his voice filled with anguish. My stomach instantly drops. A sob erupts from next to me, and I'm forced to throw my hands around her to keep her from collapsing.

"No! NO!" she wails, and Trevor rushes to her.

"She's alive. She was poisoned. That motherfucker poisoned her."

We both look at Trevor in confusion. "Who?" I ask first.

"Fucking Wheeler. He drugged her. He was saying some fucking weird shit about her belonging to him and him releasing her. I don't fucking know. He wasn't making sense. Why would he even do this to her? And then give us the means to save her?"

I struggle to understand some of his explanation, because he's mumbling so bad under his words. I've never seen him cry, but I sit there in shock as I watch heavy tears stream down his face. Katie, I learned is her name, jumps up, wraps her arms around him, and together, they break down.

At some point, Cam wakes up, sitting board-still next to me. I can't take my eyes off the two in front of me, though. I don't know what to do. It almost feels wrong to continue to stare at their very personal moment, but for some fucked up reason, I can't stop feeling the strong need to comfort her.

Katie.

She's nobody to me, but I want to rip her out of Trevor's arms and hold her. Kiss away her tears and tell her everything is going to be okay.

"Mr. Blackstone?"

We all snap toward the voice, finding the doctor standing

near.

"Yes, is she...?"

"She seems to be reacting to the dose. She's starting to wake up."

Trevor pulls away from Katie, but grabs her hand, and I stand there and watch as they both run through the hospital doors. Just before they fully shut, Katie turns, and her eyes find mine. I watch as she mouths, "Thank you," just as the doors shut close them.

I check my watch again, wondering where the fuck my guy is. I hate waiting. Every second he's late, I'm taking it out of his pay. If it didn't sound like he had a solid lead, I would've been gone already. I'm a Pearson. I wait for no one.

I'm sitting at an old diner just off Route 127. It hangs over the ocean, giving tourists a great view of the water while they indulge in greasy diner food. Fried fish is on special, which means I'm going to walk out of here smelling like a damn grease pit. Not even the best dry cleaner will be able to get the smell of fish out of this suit. I start tugging at my neckline of my dress shirt. The temperature today is hotter than normal. I should have gone with a blazer. *Where the fuck is this guy?* I just want this over with. I want everyone to know the truth and for Trevor to be gone. I stare out onto the beach as the smell of fish and memories suck me back down a path I fight to go.

"So, you're the big, bad, wild Pearson son, huh?" I look away from the pool, a place that used to always be filled with friends and family, but is now empty, to see Katie taking a seat in the lawn chair next to me. She finally knows who I am—who I truly am—and I wish I could have stayed the mystery man who helped her that day in the waiting room. Not the big, bad monster I'm sure everyone's painted me as.

I haven't seen her since the hospital two weeks ago. In place of her sadness and swollen face is a soft smile that makes my dick jolt. I've never seen someone with such powerful green eyes before. Would she think I was a creep if I stuck my hand out just to graze her face?

I'm curious why she's here. She's probably here with Lucy since Trevor called a family meeting to help figure out what to do about the fucking house since it's been over seven months since Dad died. I just want to burn the fucking place down. But then the thought of lighting that match reminds me why I can't seem to let it go. It feels like just yesterday this place was alive with family and friends, swimming and barbecuing. Everyone was happy. Hell, even after Dad died, I tried to keep the tradition alive with my wild parties, but none of them felt real.

I bring my eyes back to the pool in major need of a cleaning.

It's been a couple weeks since all the fucked-up shit happened with Jax, the baby, and Lucy. If Jax hadn't had a change of heart, Lucy would have been as good as dead.

Everything has been so messed up. Brock ran off with Ethan for some music festival like nothing ever happened. I've tried to talk to him and get him to tell me what's going on inside his head, but he always blows me off. He has Ethan, and they share a bond I may not ever understand. I think about Nixon. How he's stepped up for Rowan. Anything I ever felt seemed juvenile. She was right when she said I just wanted what I couldn't have. I didn't claim her years ago because I knew we wouldn't be good together. She needs someone like Nix who will devote everything to her. She deserves him. I was all about the flesh, and we could have fucked, but afterward, I would've gotten bored and broke her heart just like I did her best friend's.

Fuck, I'm a prick.

"You don't talk much, do you?"

I turn back to look at her. God, she's beautiful. I know I need to say something soon or my staring will become creepy. "I just have nothing to say." I turn back to the pool and try to concentrate on anything other than her lips. My dreams, ever since that day in the hospital, when they aren't nightmares, are filled with her and those lips wrapped around my cock.

"That's strange. All anyone around here says is what a hotshot you are. Never stop talking about how great you are. Are you great, Hayden Pearson?"

I turn back, finding her green eyes filled with mischief. She's a lot different from the last time I saw her. Her smile wasn't there before as it is now, lighting up her face. It almost allows me to forget the fucked-up new life I'm stuck in. "Would you like to find out just how great I am, Miss...?"

Her sudden blush is cute. "It's Fairchild, but you can just call me Katie."

I can't help but join her in smiling. There's something about her that makes me forget—makes me want to be someone better. "All right then. Would you like to experience the greatness of Hayden Pearson, Katie?" *I say her name low, with intent. Her rosy cheeks indicate she knows exactly what*

I'm getting at.

She turns so she's sitting on her side and rests her head on the chair. "You know, Hayden Pearson, I'm gonna be real honest with you. I have a feeling you're not as big, bad, and wild as they say you are."

"I thought they said I was great."

"Well, yes. At being big, bad, and wild. I just thought to leave that part out to be polite. But for some reason, I feel like that's just a cover. I think behind those blue eyes, you really are just great."

She stuns me silent. I fail at a quick, witty comeback. I have no reply to keep her riding my game. Instead of thanking her for saying something kind—a kindness that hasn't been shown to me for quite some time—I throw my back onto the chair and fixate my eyes on the pool again. "Yeah...well, beware, my bark truly is as big as my bite."

Instead of scaring her off, she laughs. The sound filters through the backyard, almost giving life back into the place. "Well, before you bite me, which I'm not saying no to, I wanted to say thank you. For being there for me. I wouldn't have made it through those hours without you." She reaches for my hand and squeezes. It startles me at first, the affection—something I'm not used to—then I turn to her, and her kind eyes stare back at me.

I've been with countless women. Even at such a young age. But none of them have turned my skin as hot as she's doing right now. The more fucked up thing is: I'm not even thinking about fucking her. I'm thinking about what she would do if I grabbed her, pulled her onto my lap, and held her against me.

"There you go again."

"Go where?" I ask.

"In your head. Wanna talk about it?"

I immediately shut down. My eyes are back on the pool as if it's my safety zone.

"That's fine. How about I just do what someone did for me once? It was a real life saver."

"Oh? And what was that?" I reply, a little less friendly.

She lifts our still connected hands. "This." She drops our

hands, cuddles into the seat, and joins me in staring at the pool.

I shake off the memory, though it feels more like a dream since it was so long ago. A time when I wasn't so cold and rigid toward life. But so much has happened since that day at the pool. I'm not the same. I'm sure she's not either. I look at the time and realize I've been sitting here for almost forty-five minutes. I get up and leave the diner. I rip off my suit coat and toss it into the dumpster before getting into my car and racing back toward downtown Tampa.

THREE ———————

K A T I E

"**U**NCLE TREVOR!" I SCREAM, KNOWING HE hates it when I make jokes about his age. He's technically old enough to be my dad, but *my* dad sure doesn't look as fine and fit as he does. I jump at him, forcing him to fumble with his phone and catch me.

"Jesus, woman," he scoffs, pretending he's not happy to see me. He tries to resist, but then gives in and hugs me tightly.

"This is a nice surprise! I was expecting Luce and my favorite goddaughter."

Lucy may own Trevor's heart, but their daughter, Eva, is the boss of her daddy.

About a year and a half ago, Lucy almost died. It was the scariest moment of my life. Even more so, Trevor's.

He didn't waste another second. Vowing to always protect her, he put the biggest ring on her finger and married her. I would have put up a bigger stink that he didn't wait for us to plan the coolest wedding known to man, but I was just thankful I was there to witness such an amazing moment.

Shortly after came the announcement about Eva, and nine months later, she gave birth to the sweetest, most adorable little girl, which they named her after Lucy's Gran.

"First off, I told you to stop calling me uncle. I'm not that old, dammit," Trevor grumbles, and sets me down. He grabs for the bag strap falling off my shoulder. "Lucy's stuck at work. She asked me to come get you so no one tries to kidnap you and keep you all for themselves. Her words." I laugh at how on point that is. Totally something Lucy would say.

"Well, thanks! And where is my little boo bear? She off on dates already?" I ask about their three-month-old daughter.

Another stressful look from Trevor. "No, she's at home with the nanny. And let's not mention dating. I already have her registered for the convent."

Awww, poor Trevor. Since he had a son with his prior wife, he had no idea about the scary truth of having a girl. He swears he's sending her to the nunnery as soon as she's old enough, so no boy ever dares look her way. "Got it. Nun Eva. So, did you bring the Maserati or the Porsche? I was really looking forward to being picked up in the pink Maserati." He shakes his head at the mention of Lucy's pink car, as if he's annoyed by her choice in color. Girl could have anything, and she picks pink. Only Lucy.

He gestures toward the exit and leads us out of the airport. "I have the Porsche. Lucy drove the Maserati to work thinking she was the one who was going to get you." At that, we both look at each other and laugh. Gonna have to request a raincheck on the sweet pink car ride.

As we pull out onto the freeway, I take in my surroundings. Every time I come back to Tampa, I forget how much I miss it. The smell of the salt water in the air, the sound of the waves crashing, the sun, and yeah...the sun. Back home in Minnesota, we see sun, but it's not as beautiful as it is here. Peaceful almost. We also don't have beaches, hot beach dudes, or fancy summer drink menus at all our local beach shacks.

"So, how's work? Still makin' the billions, makin' it rain?" I do the "make it rain" motion, spreading all my imaginary dollar bills across the car. I actually get a chuckle out of Trevor, which deserves a pat on the back for me.

"If that's what you want to call it, yes. Four Fathers is doing exceptionally well. Even after all the headaches."

"Awww, not cool! No one gives my Uncle Trevor lip! Who's the headache?"

"Fucking Hayden—as always."

I instantly freeze at the name. Trevor catches himself. "I'm sorry. I shouldn't have—I shouldn't have mentioned his name."

"Oh, ah...nah, it's cool. That's all history. No harm done." But the smile that left my face tells another story.

"Katie..."

"No, it's fine. I can't pretend he doesn't exist." I throw a fake smile back on my face. "But for real. I'm okay. Whatever was between us is over. I can hear his name. I can probably see him on the street and wave." Probably the biggest lie ever. "Don't hold back on my account. I'm here for you and Lucy. It's gonna be great." I know Trevor wants to say more. He's witnessed more than a handful of mine and Hayden's fights. The countless number of times toward the end where he was forced to watch as I cried in Lucy's arms over my broken heart. God, how can he *not* want to say more?

I lean forward and play with the radio, finding a song and turning it up, making it impossible for Trevor to mention anything else. I offer him another kind smile and bring my eyes and thoughts to the ocean.

Fifteen months ago...

"Okay, if I win, you go in the pool topless."

"What! No way. What if I win? What do you do?"

Hayden winks at me, causing my belly to do that little dance again. "If I lose, I'll make your wildest dreams come true and lose my boardshorts. But you have to behave. Be nice to him. He's been wanting to say hi all morning, and if you stare at him the way you're staring at me now, I'm gonna have to warn you, he's gonna want you to pet him."

My mouth falls open as he catches me off guard. Before I'm able to react, he tackles me and throws us both into the pool. I quickly suck in air just as we go under. Our eyes seem to open at the same time. Maybe it's because I'm used to this—him bringing me under the water where it's quiet, where the sounds of life and madness aren't heard. I think he does this to feel as if he doesn't have a billion-pound weight on his shoulders.

Where there's no one demanding things from him. Our eyes connect as they always do, and even under water, I feel the pull. Somehow, a complete stranger convinced me to turn my two-week stay into going on three months. But time's up, and I have to go back.

The funny thing is Hayden Pearson is far from a stranger now. He may just be everything. He looks at me under the water as if no one can touch us. If we could stay under forever, I think he would. Lucy and Trevor both warn me not to get close to him. He's a Pearson, and they tend not to be what a nice girl like myself is looking for. But what makes them think I'm a nice girl?

I look into his eyes. He looks almost at peace, his young age of twenty-one showing through. I may be five years older at twenty-seven, but I have my life together as much as a fifteen-year-old does. As I always like to remind myself, age doesn't matter. Look at Lucy and Trevor. They seem to work out.

The look of sadness etches his face when he knows our lungs need refilled with air and our quiet moment is up. With his hands still wrapped around my waist, he pushes back up and breaks through the surface.

"Hayden Pearson, I didn't want to get my hair wet."

He swims us over to the edge of the pool, pushes my back up against the pool wall, and presses himself into me. Every time he does this, its sends me a little bit more over the edge. Lowering his head, he stops just before our lips touch.

"And I didn't want to fall in love with a girl from Minnesota, but shit happens. Now, kiss me and tell me you'll stay here with me forever."

The fight to keep the tears at bay is almost impossible. Every time we're alone like this, he opens my heart up more and more for him. His kind words. His gentle caresses. The times where the cold, untouchable Pearson son doesn't exist.

"I told you I had to go home some time. I have a job. An apartment. I can't leave my brother forever. Come home with me. Let Trevor and the other partners run Four Fathers."

The strain is back in his brows. He pulls away, throwing his hands through his wild hair. "If I could do that, I would *have already. Just forget I asked. It's getting late, and I know you gotta pack. We should get out." He begins to swim away as I call for him. My voice is filled with sadness. I would do anything to stay here with him in our little bubble we've created, but there's something deep, deep down that tells me Hayden isn't ready. He may love me, as I do him. He may feel he needs me, the solace I bring him. But I can't be his scapegoat in life, and right now, I feel like that's what I am to him.*

It's only been three months, and my heart knows what it wants, but it also knows if I stay, we wouldn't last.

He doesn't stop or turn around. He continues to climb out of the pool and walk away.

I ended up staying another year.

"We're here."

I snap out of my memory to realize we're in Lucy and Trevor's driveway. "Oh shit, sorry. My mind was somewhere else I guess." He nods as if he understands, and we both climb out of his car. The front door flies open, and Lucy comes running toward me.

"My boo!" I yell, tackling her. We do our girly thang and jump up and down while squealing like little school girls. "God, girl, I've missed you." I gush at how great she looks.

"I missed you too. Man, I forgot how pasty you are," she teases, forgetting she was just as pasty three years ago.

"I know. That's why I didn't even bring a bathing suit. Need to tan e-v-e-r-y-t-h-i-n-g!" We both laugh as Trevor walks by us huffing and puffing. "What, Uncle Trev? Darlene told me tan lines are so outdated." Lucy laughs and slaps me on the shoulder. "Shhh...no mention of Darlene. She may have fed me too many vodka lemonades last weekend and got me to skinny dip in the ocean again."

I laugh out loud, and Trevor grumbles louder. Trevor's ex is a riot. I met her my first time out here, and we clicked right off the bat. I think it's cool as shit they all get along. At first, I thought it was super awkward, but five minutes in Darlene's presence, and it all clicked.

"Ladies, dinner reservations are at nine at Flemings. And, Katie? This time don't convince my wife not to wear underwear. If she tries to save the lobsters again and I have to carry her out, I'd appreciate the entire restaurant not getting a view of what's mine. I don't want to have to murder anyone." With that, Trevor walks into their gigantic mansion.

"Your husband is super-hot when he's bossy," I say, grabbing my bag and following her into their home.

Lucy turns back to me, and with a smile as big as someone who just won the lottery, she says, "I know."

FOUR

H A Y D E N

"**A**ND YOU'RE FUCKING SURE THIS TIME?"

"All the dots connect. I'm sure."

I'm sitting at the table of my condo, staring down at the information Wyatt Brandon just gave me. And of course, my suspicions were right. "And this confirms Jameson Vincent is indeed Trevor Blackstone?"

Wyatt nods, but looks unsure. Goddammit. "Is it or not?"

"The paper trail of funds all lead back to Mr. Blackstone. This guy, your Jameson Vincent, he's like a ghost, if that's his real name, but he isn't in the records. If I had to make a professional guess, I don't think that's your guy, but they are connected in some way."

A professional guess? *A professional guess!*

"I've spent the last four months searching for the truth and you're coming at me with a guess?" Slamming my fists down, I shove my chair back, walk over to the wall-to-wall window overlooking the city, and thrust my hand through my hair.

"Hayden—"

"It's Mr. Pearson to you. I pay you enough money, you will respect who I am."

"Yes, of course, Mr. Pearson. We've gone over these many times. And each time, I come back with the same information. Trevor Blackstone has been sending money to an account with the name Jameson Vincent. The only puzzle piece was how he was connected to Jameson Vincent. The locations Jameson has been spotted don't match up with Trevor's business trips. I am confident they are not one person. But the money trail leads me to conclude they know one another."

I grip my hair so tight, it's gonna cause a headache. *What the fuck were you up to, Mom?* A question I won't ever get answered. I thought I had him. I was going to finally ruin his life the way he ruined our family.

"Get out."

"What about my mone—"

"GET OUT!" I yell, watching from the reflection of the dark night as Mr. Brandon jumps from his seat, grabs his coat, and scurries out my door.

"FUCK!" I scream. This wasn't supposed to be the outcome. Everything I've done. It was supposed to lead up to him being gone and finally out of my brothers' lives. I won't let losing everything—losing *her*—be for nothing.

Three months ago...

"Hayden, you have to let this go. This is not healthy."

I take a swig from the bottle of my eighteen-year Macallan aged scotch. Dear old dad's favorite. "You know what's not healthy? My girlfriend not taking my side. Taking his side." Another swig. I stumble, almost falling into the pool. Katie screams in fear, but I catch myself and toss myself into the lawn chair.

"You have to stop. I can't stick around and watch you obsess over this ridiculous theory any longer." My arm is up, and the bottle of scotch is flying through the air, shattering against the stone wall. Too close to her. She screams again, the sound mingling with her cries.

I cringe thinking I could have almost hurt her, but my anger doesn't subside. "I'm not fucking wrong. That motherfucker is lying. Everyone thinks he's a fucking saint. He's not. He's a fucking scam artist out for our money, and he's Nixon's father. I know it. I can prove it."

I don't need her to say it to know how disappointed she is in me. It's written all over her face. She's done with me. I can feel it. Her hands fly up in the air, getting just as worked up as I am.

"Give me a break, Hay. He has his own fortune, why would he need yours? And why would him being Nixon's father be so bad? Trevor is a great man. He has done nothing but care *for Nixon. Shown him love, support—"*

"STOP! Fucking stop! Shut the fuck up." My voice startles her, but why does she not understand? The only person I love in this goddamn fucking world and she doubts me.

I'm up and storming toward her. I would never hurt her, but she doesn't seem to know that. She flinches when I get close, and it guts me even more.

"You need to see someone, Hay. You're obsessed. Is this because Nixon gets to feel what it's like to have a dad? A father figure who loves him?"

"Shut up."

"Are you angry because your father never showed you that kind of love?"

"Shut the fuck up, Katie."

"No! Look what you've become because of this! You're so angry. The drinking. And now? What are you going to do? Hit me? I'm done, Hay. God, I stayed. I stayed for you. I left everything because you swore you loved me. But this..." She raises her hands to the house. Eric's house. "You're choosing

to continue to live in this hell. Look around you. Everyone else has moved on from the past. Your brothers have moved on. But you? You're still stuck in a world where Eric Pearson rules you. He was an awful dad, I get it, but you need to move on. Why do you still have this house? Huh? It brings you nothing but misery. Bad memory after bad memory."

"I stay because of my brother."

"Which brother? Nixon wants nothing to do with this place. Neither does Brock. They won't judge you if you sold it. And Camden's here because of you. Because you're his guardian. No one is holding you here. Let it go. Let your hatred for your father go. Let the hatred for Trevor go. Move on—"

"I CAN'T MOVE ON! I can't. And you know what? Yes, I fucking despise Trevor. Maybe even a part of me feels the same way about Nixon. I was the oldest. I endured way more of the bullshit my father put us through. And all anyone can do is pretend Eric Pearson didn't exist and Trevor is father step-in of the year."

Katie takes a calculated step toward me. "I love you.

Trevor loves you. Let him help you."

I'm ashamed for my reaction, but the liquor takes over. My hands go up and wrap around Katie's shoulders harder than I should. I begin to shake her. I need the lies she speaks to stop. I need her to understand. I need her to know how it feels inside me. The hole. The anger.

"Hayden, stop, you're hurting me!"

Oh god, what am I doing? I've crossed the line. How will she forgive me for this? My eyes begin to sting. The gut wrenching guilt sets in as her sobs break through. Before I snap out of my haze, my hands are ripped off her and I'm tossed into the pool. I fall in, hoping I never come up. I just want to stay in the quietness of the water until there's no more air left in my lungs.

Hands are around my waist, and I'm brought to the surface. I start gasping for air, but fight the person holding me for bringing me back up to the surface of the hell I'm living.

"Get the fuck off me!" I growl.

"Not until you calm down." Camden. Fuck. I don't want him to see me like this.

My wild eyes search the deck, landing on Katie. God, my beautiful Katie. What have I done? I want to jump out and go to her. Tell her I'm sorry. Beg her to forgive me. Not to leave me. But I know she's going to. I saw the packed bags earlier today.

Then my eyes roam to the person consoling her. Trevor. My rage returns, and I'm blinded, unable to stop myself.

"You know what? Fine. You don't want to be here, then leave. Fucking leave. Why don't you have Trevor take you home. Maybe he can fuck you too."

The immediate pain in her eyes tears me apart, but the liquor inside me won't stop.

"Hayden, chill, man," Camden says, still trying to keep hold of me. Trevor wraps his arm around Katie, and I erupt. I throw my head back, knocking into Camden's nose with a crack. He releases me, and I don't even bother looking to see if he's okay. I jump out of the pool and run for Trevor.

"Get the fuck off my property. And take her with you."

I don't get anything else out because Trevor turns around and socks me. My head flies back, and I stumble, almost landing in the pool.

"You will regret this, son. I suggest you shut that mouth of yours."

I bounce back, taking a swing, but he blocks it and takes another hit to my stomach.

"Trevor, stop!" Katie sobs from behind him.

"Trevor, your girlfriend wants you to stop—"

Another hit to the ribs. This time, I bend forward, trying to catch my breath.

"You mean your girlfriend, you dumb fuck up. You don't want my help, fine. But I warned you about hurting her. Now, you're done. Regret is a heavy load to bear, son. I hope you realize that and find a way out of whatever darkness you're stuck under. And when you do, I hope you still have people around you for support, 'cause this one's gonna hurt."

"GET OUT! GET THE FUCK OFF MY PROPERTY!" I yell and scream and cuss. I take chairs and toss them with all my might. Trevor cradles my sobbing girlfriend—the only person who's ever truly loved me—under

his arm and walks her off my property and out of my life.

I woke up the next morning alone, with a busted nose and a bruised ribcage. Katie was gone. It took me some time to put the pieces together. Remember the things I said. I made an effort to reach out to her, but she wasn't having it. She went back home, and that was that. The only time in my entire life I felt alive, loved, was gone.

That was the last time I spoke to Katie. She did a great job of dodging me. It seemed Cam kept in contact with her, though. That's how I knew Lucy went to visit her shortly after instead of her returning here. I figured I had something to do with that since I knew Katie loved the beach and the sun.

I lost everything because I couldn't let something that had nothing to do with me go. It was then I knew I had nothing else to lose. So, I shut down and gave everyone the Hayden they expected. Just as Katie once described me: the big, bad, and wild Pearson son.

I spent the last three months running Four Fathers just like my father, the big bad wolf. I ran with groups older than me. Lost myself in drugs and partying. I spent more money on materialistic things I never even opened the boxes to than some spend in their lifetime. I just didn't give a fuck.

Because that's who I was.

That's who I am.

FIVE ————

K A T I E

"**O**H MY GOD, YES! I REMEMBER! AND YOU WERE trying to make out with Jimmy Wallace but ended up getting sick and barfing all over his Camaro."

Lucy and I both burst out laughing at the college memory. Lucy was a sophomore, and I was a freshman. We met at one of the school keggers and instantly hit it off.

"Oh, so our wedding and puking in the limo wasn't the first time you destroyed a vehicle?" Trevor pokes, and Lucy laughs harder.

"Hey! I apologized for that like a million times over! It's not my fault your guests know how to party and overserved me."

I know I have a smile on my face, because it *was* true. Those Pearson boys sure knew how to get down. But it's one Pearson in particular my mind suddenly goes to.

"May I have this dance?"

I turn to see Hayden, looking so damn handsome in his suit. He's such a sight. I should be used to seeing him in suits now, but tonight, he takes my breath away. "I believe I can spare a dance for you."

He takes my hand and brings me out onto the small, lit dancefloor. Trevor and Lucy transformed the private beach into a beautiful scene from A Midsummer Night's Dream. The full moon shines bright in the perfect night sky, along with the lights draping in waves above us. The quartet plays a slow melody as Hayden spins me in the middle of the floor.

"This is going to be us one day, you know," he says, bringing our bodies close together. His words stun me. It's only been a few weeks, and I know we're moving fast. The way I feel for him scares me. It's so powerful, sometimes when I look at him, I fear he's not real. There's no doubt he doesn't feel the same. The words he confesses are strong with meaning, I fight not to cry. He's incredibly intense. Like a force I have no chance

of running from even if I try. I'm in love with him, and it's so deep, it almost hurts. "Are you going to say something or let me suffer?"

"What makes you think you want to marry a girl like me?" I try to coat my answer, hoping he doesn't feel the erratic beat of my heart.

He spins me again, and I laugh when he dips me, placing a kiss to my lips. He brings me up and answers, "Because it's just my destiny to. You're the one. You know it, I know it. My heart is home with you."

He smiles down at me as he wipes the tear that's fallen down my cheek.

"I love you, Katie. You're my angel. My life. And whether you like it or not, one day, you will be my—"

"What the fuck, enough dancing!" Hayden's brother interrupts our moment. Before he finishes his sentence, we turn to Brock. "Dude, let's go. It's time for shots. Lots of shots..."

"Well, if I would have known the ice sculptures were going to turn into shot luges, I may have thought twice about ordering them," Trevor chimes in, bringing me back to the present. I never answered Hayden's question that night. We were indeed pulled off the dancefloor and the shot competition began. I'm not even sure why I was the only one called out for puking when I know for a fact Brock vomited all over the gift table and blamed it on Trevor's son.

"I promise not to make a habit of it. Your Maserati is safe from me tonight." I wink and take a huge gulp, finishing off my fourth martini. "So, what's on the agenda while I'm here? No kinky sex. I can tell when you two get kinky. Luce over here walks funny."

"Katie!" Lucy laughs, hitting me with her napkin.

"What? It's true! And then you two spend the whole next day with your little inside jokes. Daddy this, babysitter that...for real..."

Trevor picks up his hand to flag down the waiter while Lucy and I bust out laughing harder. "Okay, I'll stop. Don't make us go home. We'll be good. I promise,"

I drunkenly plead.

Trevor eyes his wife, trying to feel her out. He's been this way ever since the incident. What Jaxson Wheeler did not only took a toll on Lucy, but Trevor too. Her depression got worse. His counting almost destroyed them. But I guess love just has a way of holding you together until you're ready to be okay. *Ughhh love.* I hate that word. I hate hearing it. Thinking it. Still feeling it.

"You okay there?"

I look to Trevor. "Yeah, of course. Why wouldn't I be?"

"You just looked like you went somewhere again."

I don't want to admit it, but my wounds still bleed at the broken heart Hayden left me with. There are still times when I find myself in tears at the way we ended things. How he didn't care enough to fight for us. He let me walk out. But in the end, I only blame myself. I knew from the beginning I shouldn't have stayed. But I did. And he ended up ruining us just as I predicted.

"Nope, all good. One stop. Let's go to Clybourne's

for a quick dance, then you can take your wifey home and do nasty things to her while I raid your fridge and watch one of your three thousand movie channels."

Trevor smiles and looks at his wife. "Please, Daddy? I won't break curfew..." Lucy leans in closer and lowers her voice, but since she's drunk, she's still loud enough for half the restaurant to hear. "Or maybe I will, and you'll have to spank me."

The old woman behind us gasps in horror as I choke on my sip of water. Trevor pulls out his wallet and throws an impressive wad of cash on the table without even seeing the bill. He abruptly stands, pulling Lucy up with him. "One dance, then this ass is mine," he says, slapping Lucy's ass. She squeals in delight and grabs my hand to walk toward the exit of the restaurant.

"Trevor, again, thank you. That meal was amazing."

"Anything for my girls."

Obnoxious giggling has us pulling our attention to the couple walking in.

"I can just eat you up."

I hear the words, and they register before the voice does. I look up, and my eyes collide with his.

"God, you're beautiful. I feel like I can't say that enough." Nip after nip. Lick after lick, Hayden kisses every part of my skin. My back arches off his feathered comforter when his warm mouth covers my breast. "I just can't stop. I'm going to eat you all up."

I start to laugh. "I didn't know you were into that kind of kinky shit, Mr. Pearson. Sex, bondage, and flesh eating?"

His teeth wrap around my nipple, and he bites down, sending my head back. "I would be if it meant being closer to you. That's how bad I need you. You're mine, you know that, right? Every single fucking part of you." He sucks hard, then releases me and works his way to my other breast. "Anyone else ever thinks of having what's mine, I'll kill 'em."

I laugh again at his fierce words. Hayden loves to come across so scary, but inside, he's just a big cuddly bear. "I think I can handle that."

"Good. Now, I'm going to need to fuck you hard. Then sweet. Then hard as fuck again. Hold on tight, baby..."

He's still staring at me when I come to from the past. His eyes are dark and intense. Lucy puts her arm around me for comfort as Trevor steps forward, becoming a blockade between us.

"Well, look who the cat dragged in," Hayden says, his arm around a tall blonde, fake from head to toe.

"Hayden," Trevor addresses him, but says no more. I know he's on alert for my sake.

Hayden stares him down, and if looks could kill... It tells me nothing has changed in the last three months. My heart hurts knowing he hasn't let go. It's evident in his stiff posture, and the way he's starting to grip his floozy date too hard.

"Trevor, didn't take you for a sharer, but more the merrier, I suppose."

Lucy takes a step toward him. "Screw off, Hayden,"

she snaps, but Trevor throws his hand out to stop her.

He just laughs back. "Hard pass, Luce. I'm not into group sharing, unlike your husband, I see." He pulls his eyes away from her to me. They're sharp and cold. I inhale a deep breath of air at the way he's looking at me. My body reacts to him being so close. As if no time has passed. I hate him and love him just the same. The alcohol isn't to blame for the temperature rising in my body. The tingles of remembering his hands on me. His mouth— once so sweet and loving, now trying and succeeding at being hurtful.

"Katie," he says my name, but it's not sweet or endearing. There's no sense of longing in his tone. His intentions are to be cruel. I don't respond to him. Because I can't. My throat is locked. I've tried to prepare for this day. When we would see one another again. I dreamt he would fall to his knees, begging for forgiveness, and I would accept. All the pain and hurt would dissipate and we would have the life he promised us.

It's what he's doing now I feared most. Rejection. But part of me expected this. This is who he is—who he wants the world to see. I shouldn't expect him to treat me any different, because I am no different to him. He proved that three months ago when he threw me away.

"We were just leaving. Have a good meal," Trevor says, surprisingly calm. He raises his arm for us ladies to walk past them. Lucy abides and starts to walk, grabbing my hand and tugging me with her. I'm thankful, because my legs wouldn't move any other way. We pass, and the universal gods wouldn't have it otherwise. Our shoulders brush against one another, and the feeling is so light, warmth rushes down to my feet, tickling every nerve ending in my body. My legs threaten to buckle, but two strong hands wrap around me.

"Get your hands off her, asshole," Lucy hisses.

My head lifts just in time to catch the searing gaze of his steel blue eyes. He doesn't need to say anything. He can see he still has that control over me. He always has.

Since the first day we met. Our first kiss. The first time we made love. When he told me he loved me and begged me never to leave him.

Our connection is quickly broken when Lucy pulls me away. Sadly, he lets me go. I hear Trevor say goodnight, and we stumble out of the restaurant.

I take two steps, turn to my right, and bend over, throwing up my meal. As I lift my head to a set of worried eyes, I throw on my fake smile, and say, "At least it wasn't in the Maserati."

SIX

H A Y D E N

I DON'T EVEN FEEL MY FEET ANYMORE. I KNOW they're hitting pavement, but I've been running for so long, my legs have gone completely numb. I know I should stop, but my brain won't let me. I need to keep going until I get the image of her out of my head.

She looked flawless. Perfect. Sad. Not mine anymore.

My legs work faster, taking the corner of the park to the beachfront path. The sun is hours from coming up, but I know the path like the back of my hands. I could run this blindfolded.

Seeing her with Trevor cut me. A reminder of who she chose. It wasn't me. She chose to defend him and leave. She left with him. I may have overdone it, but she was supposed to be on my side. She was *my* girl. *My* life. I relay the things she said to me the night I kicked her out. All the hurtful, yet truthful things about my father. She was right. With all of them. And maybe I just didn't want to accept them.

Maybe, deep down, I did loathe Nixon for having something I wish I had. He had someone in his life who genuinely cared about him, whereas I had a man whose only concern was grooming me to be his prodigy. I didn't plan on touching Four Fathers. I wanted to leave Tampa and never look back. He knew that. So he made sure even after death he still had total control over me.

If he knew what a backstabbing friend Trevor was, I wonder if he would have wanted his shares to go to him. Knowing my father, his only motto would have been to destroy. No one crossed the great Eric Pearson. Maybe that's the reason. It's the Pearson blood that runs through me, that refuses to let this die.

I should have exposed Trevor last night at the restaurant. I humiliated him in one of Tampa's most elite restaurants. I'm sure half the customers in there were clients or colleagues of some sort. But I didn't expect to see her.

Mine.

I dig my feet into the sand and push myself harder than I ever have. The morning dew allows me to dig deep and push off hard with each pounding stride. I can already tell it's going to be hot, with the early morning thickness in the air.

The way she looked at me wasn't any less painful than a knife being shoved deep into my chest. Angry, sad. I wanted to grab her and throw her into my arms. But the quick glimpse she took at the nobody on my arm ruined it. She shut down and that look that secretly asked me to make it better disappeared.

We never sat down for dinner.

I went to the bar and ordered two shots of scotch. Fed one to my date and one to myself, then I put her in a cab and left. I drove to the old house that still sits empty because I can't bring myself to accept an offer and killed myself some more by sitting by the pool rehashing all the good and bad memories.

A part of me always thought Katie would come back. She promised she'd never leave me. And she was a woman who kept her promises. But time passed, and without contact, the hardness in me grew. She fucking lied. Because she sure as hell left me.

The anger, as if it were just yesterday, begins to rebuild. One after another, my feet smack onto the moist sand, until I can no longer push forward. My legs buckle and my knees smash into the ground. Fuck her. Fuck Trevor. Fuck everyone. I'm done. I'm taking him down now.

———

Four days later...

An issue with the Cleveland transports delays me from the office for four days. A company decided last minute they weren't ready to sell, which demanded my presence in Ohio to convince them they were indeed ready to fucking sell.

I finally walk into Four Fathers on a mission.

"Is Blackstone in?" I ask the receptionist.

"He sure is, *Hayden*. He's in his office."

I storm past, but halt, whipping around to her. "It's Mr. Pearson. Know who you work for...and take that red crap off your lips or leave. This isn't a whore house." I turn, not bothering with her reaction, my feet slamming down the hallway as I hit Trevor's office, throwing open his door.

"I see knocking isn't something that applies to you," Trevor says. He's not the only one in the office. Sitting on his desk is Lucy, and to the right is Katie.

"Clear the room. I need to talk to your master."

Trevor's eyes light up. He begins to stand, preparing his defense. "I suggest you watch your tone. This is still my company as well, and I will not stand here and take shit from a fucking punk like you."

"Fuck you, Blackstone. You're done here."

His fists slam on his desk. "I'm over putting up with your shit. Your father may have been my best friend, but I've had enough of you."

Fuck him. "Good, because this is the end of the road for you, asshole."

Katie slides off the desk. "Jesus, Hayden, stop this!"

"Shut the fuck up and mind your own fucking business. This has nothing to do with you," I snap, my eyes shooting daggers of betrayal at her. I pull them away and lock them back on my enemy.

"Spit out what it is you want and get the fuck out of here."

I toss the file onto his desk. "I want to talk about Jameson Vincent." Trevor's eyes go wide. *Fucking got you, asshole.* His body stiffens at the name, and I know I've won. Lucy looks confused and turns to her husband.

"Who is Jameson Vincent?" she asks. She's about to find out.

"I need a moment with Hayden. Alone," Trevor says, his tone blank. Lucy looks as if she's going to argue but thinks twice. She nods to Katie, who I refuse to make eye contact with, and they exit his office.

"You can thank my mother and her fondness for holding onto memories for ruining your perfect plan." I toss the old photo on his desk. He picks it up and eyes it, flipping it over to the back, then back to the front. "As they say, a picture is worth a thousand words. The day in the hospital, when I mentioned the paternity test for Nixon, you looked shocked—yet you were the one who had that fucking manipulated. I found the real one, motherfucker."

Trevor drops the picture and sits back in his chair. "What do you know?"

Is he fucking kidding me right now? He's not even going to deny it? "I know everything, you motherfucker. I know all the lies, the fake identity, the money transferring. I know you are, in fact, Nixon's father."

Twice now, I catch him in a shocked stare. "Is this what you've been obsessing over? All these months? Wasting your life, ruining everything? For *this*?" He thrusts the papers across the desk and they fall off the ledge in front of my feet.

"Ruining? I'm exposing the truth. Your lies. How did it start? Did you and my mom meet in college? On the streets? Did you conjure up this scam back then to befriend my father with the plan to eventually take what was rightfully his?"

"You have it all wrong, son."

I rush forward and slam my palms on his desk, causing him to jump up. "I am not your GODDAMN SON! But this proves Nixon is."

"You have it wrong," Trevor repeats, and red filters my vision.

"No, asshole, that's one thing I have *right*. You're going down, Blackstone. I want you out of here by today. I'll give you a few hours to pack your shit and hide before I tell the entire world and your family what a con artist you are." I turn my back and head to the door when his words hit me.

"You're right. That man in the photo is Nixon's father. That's the only thing you do have right."

I stop and turn, though I'm not sure why I'm even giving him stage time to talk himself out of this. "Your father did his diligence when starting this company. He wanted to know anything in my past wasn't going to ruin an ounce of what we were creating, so he had an investigator look into my background."

"And?" I growl.

"And he didn't find much, apart from some uncle only twelve years older than me. He was just getting out of prison for some DUI at the time. He's a gambler, not someone I wanted in my life or around my family—*you guys*—but your mother found the information years later in your dad's files and couldn't leave it alone. She felt sorry for me being alone, so she sought him out."

"I don't believe you. I used to watch the way my mother looked at you. Flirted with you."

"Hayden, your mother had issues, we all fucking know that. She flirted with anyone who gave her some attention. And that ain't my problem. Despite what you think of me, I wouldn't sleep with another man's wife—especially my best fucking friend's."

I throw my hands through my hair, my agitation growing. He's lying. He's lying. "You're not going to convince me of this bullshit. I know about the money! I have fucking proof!"

"Proof of what? That I send him money? So fucking what? I do it to protect Nixon, and before he died, I was protecting your father. Your mother came to me about Nixon when she was worried about Eric getting paternity tests done for insurance policies. She panicked, and I told her I'd help her, but Eric could never know it was me who helped her if he ever found out."

"So why are you sending him money?"

"He came here...when your mother left—or should I say disappeared? He saw a missing person's ad for her, and he saw Nixon. Just by looking at him, he knew he was his. He also knew how rich Eric was. He showed up here and I intercepted him by accident. I managed to convince him to go away. A small fee each month to keep your father from knowing about Nixon and to keep Nixon from spiraling. This will break him, Hayden."

"What about the name on the photo? Why give her a picture of him with his name?"

"Because he changed his name. He rotates between five aliases. He gets himself in debt and has some warrants for violent crimes, so he changes between names. That was his real one he always went back to."

"That's why my investigator found nothing on him," I fume.

"Actually, your investigator found me. And I convinced him not to tell you. I assumed you found the image and were curious who it was. I didn't suspect you'd come up with this whole fucking scenario that it was me."

"You fucking *what*!"

"It seems money will convince anyone to switch teams I see," he says, throwing himself back in his chair. "Hayden...I kept this from you all because it was the right thing to do. If you feel otherwise, then you do what you feel is right. But know that this information won't fix anything for you. It won't bring your dad back. It won't justify anything for you."

His words are true despite not wanting to believe them. Telling Nixon will do nothing but hurt him and bring up the past. He's the happiest I've ever seen him, and this could threaten that. And without Rowan and Erica, I don't know where he would be. His darkness far exceeds mine. It scares me most times.

"Your father loved you."

"He didn't love anyone," I spit. "He only loved *you*." Uncle Trevor. That's who he showed the most affection to. He may have acted hard and collective, but Trevor was his best friend. His brother, his partner. When my mom left, he was his rock. He didn't lean on his children who would have loved to lean back. No, he had *him*.

"I know you only see it one way. But you have no idea how much he loved you all."

I can't be here any longer. My hands are shaking, and my throat is beginning to lock. Emotions I refuse to acknowledge are starting to boil, and I need air. "I'm done." Turning, I throw his door open, storm past the two women, and head straight into my office. I slam the door so hard, a few paintings fall from their hinges and crash to the ground. I feel like I just ran a ten-mile marathon and can't catch my breath. My eyes are stinging. I can't reel in my emotions. "Fuck him. Fuck him—"

"Hayden, are you okay?"

I whip around to see Katie standing in my office.

"What the fuck do you want? To gloat? No need. Get out." I turn back to face the windows, needing to rein in these unfamiliar feelings.

"I just want to know you're okay. I still worry about you."

Her words trigger a deep emotion I have buried so far down, it releases a darkness I try to keep caged. I turn around and rush her, barricading her between my body and the bookshelf. "You're worried about me? How so? Are you as worried as you should've been when you walked out on me? Left me like you promised you wouldn't?" Her body trembles under the force of my words.

"You drove me away, you know that."

"And you left as soon as it got tough." She tries to push me away, but I only eliminate the space left between us. Her tits are pressed against my chest and the way they brush up and down as she breathes heavily causes my cock to grow.

"I left because you were out of control. You were obsessed with a theory that didn't exist."

I lift my hand quickly and startle her. She thinks I'm going to hurt her. Her reaction fucking guts me, but thrills me all the same. I gently wrap my hand around her neck, then lower my head until I know she can feel my warm breath hitting her flushed cheek. "The only thing I was obsessed with was you." I slide my fingers down her neck, between her breasts. "You were the only thing I wanted. Needed. I thought I made that clear every moment we were together when I poured my heart out to you like a goddamn whipped pussy boy." She inhales quickly at my words. I expect her to stop my hand from traveling, but she doesn't. I move past her taut belly, past her navel and her too short skirt, until my hand is massaging her inner thigh. "Since when do you wear skirts? Thought my girl only wore shorts."

"Since I became not your girl anymore," she whispers, and her eyes fall shut as my hand works up and inside her panties. *Fuck*. Soaked. As always. I always did that to her. I should stop myself. This is just going to fuck me up by getting a little taste of her. But I was never good at keeping my hands off her.

"Hayden..."

My name is a soft whisper off her lips, followed by a sweet as fuck moan when I pull her panties aside and insert a finger inside her. I almost lose my shit the moment my finger reaches deep into her cunt. The warmth. Tightness. I can smell her sweetness. My mind is foggy, and I can't stop. I pull out and replace one finger with two. She squirms in my hold. I love how much her body succumbs to my touch. I always had that control over her. It was like a fucking drug I couldn't get enough of. I pull out and begin finger fucking her against the bookshelf. There is no lenience in my thrusts. I can't stop. I need this. Her soft moans fill my office, and it may take an army to force me not to turn her around and fuck her hard and viciously over my desk.

"Hayden..." My name again drives me mad.

"Is this what you wanted, Kitty Kat? You wanted me

to get you to purr my name as I do what I want with your cunt? Always a willing cunt. Is it still mine? Or have you been letting other men touch what belongs to me?"

Her body freezes. She lifts her hands to push me away from her, but I just slam my fingers harder inside her. "Do you think of me when other men touch you like this?" In and out, in and out.

"Hayden, stop." She pushes again, but I know what she wants. I always have. The way she's riding my hand tells me that's the last thing she wants me to do. Thank god, because I can't stop. I've lost sense of right and wrong and can't stop until I make her come and she remembers who she once belonged to. "Hayden." Her plea finally breaks through just as she squeezes around my fingers, orgasming. Realization strikes me, and I practically drop her as I pull out and throw myself a few feet away from her. We're both breathing heavily. I must look like a madman. I make the mistake of looking at her. Her eyes are glossy, the aftermath of her orgasm mixed with unshed tears.

"Just leave me alone. Don't come back here. Ever."

She doesn't say another word. For the second time, she turns and walks away from me.

SEVEN

K A T I E

One week later...

THE SUN IN TAMPA IS NO JOKE. THE TEMPERATURE doesn't faze Lucy, but since I'm not used to it, I keep having to take breaks inside and drink a gallon of water so I don't dehydrate and crinkle up. I walk inside to find Trevor in the kitchen. "Hey, aren't you supposed to be at work?" I ask, opening the fridge and grabbing a bottle of water.

"Yeah, but this week and next tend to be quiet in the office. It's the anniversary of Eric's death, so everyone kind of handles it in their own way."

"Oh yeah, I'm sorry. I should have known." I knew the anniversary was close. Mainly why I chose this time to visit. It seems to be hard for Trevor, which makes it hard for Lucy, so I want to do what I can to ease the time.

"No need to apologize. It's a hard time for a lot of people. We manage to get through it." He finishes signing some documents and starts clearing up the table.

"Hey, Trev, can I ask you something?"

"Have at it. But no more bondage talk. My ex is a liar and needs to stop filling your heads with weird shit."

I laugh. "That was actually my second question. But... how's Hayden been lately?"

He lifts his head to observe me, not happy I'm even inquiring about him. "I wouldn't know. He hasn't shown up for the past week."

What? *That* surprises me. "Why not? I thought he loved throwing his weight around at work?"

Trevor shuts his briefcase and places it on the edge of the counter. "Hayden has a rough go around during this time. I'm not surprised he's gone MIA. You've seen him at his worst. He doesn't handle certain situations well. This is one of them. Eric dying was a blessing and a curse all the same for him. He wanted to hate his father for all the lacking he did as one. He would say he was glad he was gone, but deep down, he hates him more for being gone and leaving him with the company he never wanted to run and responsible for his three brothers...even though two are of age. Being the oldest, he left a lot of baggage for him to handle. So, it's a struggle for him."

Everything Trevor says is true. Hayden was never good at expressing his feelings toward anyone but me. It seemed like I was the only person he was able to open up to. But when it came to his issues with his family, he shut down—went to that dark place he talked about only when he had too many drinks. He was troubled and lost. But he wanted to be saved so desperately.

I always thought that's why I stayed. Instead of knowing he needed to save himself, I was going to be the one to pull him from his dark place. But in the end, he just drove a bigger wedge between us. A part of me hoped me leaving would help him figure his shit out. But being back here only proves he's still broken and alone.

"I'm not sure I like the look on your face right now. Don't do anything stupid. Katie, he doesn't deserve you. He's proven that time and time again."

I won't deny that. He doesn't deserve me. But he deserves to be loved and understood. He deserves to be happy and feel at peace. And I know at one point in his life I offered him that. "I know. It's just...we all deserve something more, ya know? He can't continue being so hateful, and it hurts to see someone be so hard on themselves. We may not be right for one another, and what he did, I won't forget, but love doesn't shut off just because of our wrong doings, ya know?"

He looks at me for some time, then with nothing else to say, he nods. He understands. And he may not agree, but he accepts my decision. His last words are to be careful as he heads out back to his wife who's going to have to explain why she's sunbathing on the beach with no top.

Avoiding that shit show, I go change into a cute little summer dress and text Camden, asking for his new address. Cam and I kept in touch even after Hayden and I went our separate ways. His love for politics interested me like no other, and he promised me a tour of the White House when he made it there one day. He responds with the address, then keeps on going, asking for advice.

Cam: This watch? Or this one?

Both pictures look obnoxiously expensive.

Me: First one. Do I dare ask how much that one is?

Cam: Too much, but definitely worth it.

Me: Special occasion?

Cam: Spoiling myself is always a special occasion.

Me: You're ridiculous.

Cam: You love me. Good luck. I won't be there to run interference but call me if I need to beat his ass.

I silently thank him knowing I'm going to need it.

———

I spend thirty minutes talking myself in and out of this plan before I finally walk in and give my name to the bellman. If he wants to refuse me, that's that. A simple he's not in or does not require your presence from his fancy butler will do and I'll be on my way.

When the bellman states my name through the phone, I'm surprised Hayden allows me access. I was certain he would tell him I was an intruder and to shoot me on the spot. I thank the man and hit the button for the twenty-third floor. Each floor that reaches closer to my destination puts me in a panic. Is this a bad idea? Should I have just let it rest? Should I have gotten the hint when he gave me the best orgasm I've had in the past three months before insulting me and throwing me out of his office?

The elevator door opens to the penthouse. It's just a small hallway and door separating me and what may turn out to be a very bad decision. With a deep breath and a silent pep talk to go get him, I step off the elevator and raise my hand to knock.

The door opens before my hand ever reaches it, but no one's there. It leaves me no choice but to push it the rest of the way and walk in.

"I assume you're lost?" Hayden's voice comes from the left, and I turn to see him walking into his living room. My breath catches at his back. He's shirtless. His skin is tan and muscular. These past months have agreed with him. He's clearly been hitting the gym. More muscle. His hair is longer, but he still keeps it wild and hot.

"I...nope, right place," I say, walking farther into the place. Man, it's nice. For someone his age, he sure lives the life. "Your place is awesome," I say, not sure how else to start since he isn't even giving me his attention.

"Cam likes it," he states, as if he's not here for himself, but for his brother. When he finally turns to face me, my stomach drops.

"Hayden," I whisper his name, no hiding the anguish in my voice. He looks horrible. His eyes are dark, circles lining them. He had to have skipped every meal this week. I look around and see beer bottles littering the coffee table.

He runs his hands though his hair, making it look even more wild and unkept. He scans the sight I'm taking in. "Welcome to my life. If you have an opinion, then get the fuck out." This time, his hurtful words don't faze me. I know he's hurting. I tread slowly into the living room until I'm close enough to smell the booze on his breath.

I'm not sure if he'll let me, but I try anyway. I raise my hand and cup his cheek. His skin is clammy. My heart swells when he doesn't push me away and leans into my hand instead. "Hayden, you have to stop doing this to yourself." I can't stop the tears that begin to fall. He looks so pained. So lost. "You're not taking care of yourself." I lift my free hand to caress the other side of his face just as he raises his to wipe at my wet cheek.

"It's two years tomorrow," he says, as if he didn't hear a single word I just spoke.

"I know," I reply.

"If he were here, he'd probably be planning a huge barbeque. Cooking his damn burgers and inviting over half the town just to show off whatever new toy he just bought."

"I bet he would."

"Why are you crying?" he asks, as if I'm the one who needs nurturing.

"Because you're torturing yourself and it hurts so bad to stand by and watch you lose yourself." The tears start pouring down my face. "I'm sorry I left. If I would have just stood up to you and stuck it out, maybe you wouldn't be so broken."

Hayden grabs my face and lifts my chin, so I have no choice but to stare deep into his eyes. "You should have left me long before you did. I was never good for you."

"Yes, you were—"

"No, I wasn't. I should have cherished you. Instead, I took all my fucked-up issues out on you." He bends down, touching his forehead to mine. "I should never have forced you to stay. I was being selfish with you. I wanted you to myself. Even though I knew I wasn't in the best place. I was far from able to give you what you truly wanted. And I spent that entire year taking advantage of you."

He pulls me into his arms, and I wrap mine around him, holding on for dear life. I begin to sob, thinking of all the regret and wrong choices we've both made. Once upon a time, we were so in love. There wasn't a moment that passed when our time wasn't spent together. Our thoughts were on each other. We had our rough patches like any other couple, but ours were different. We shared a bond so many couples never get to share. He had his demons. I knew that. I didn't go into our relationship blind. But my tears are for allowing them to get between us.

"Stop crying," he whispers into my hair, but it only makes me cry harder. That's when I feel my feet being lifted and I'm in his arms. He carries me over to the couch and sits us down with me on his lap, allowing me to break down for the both of us. I know he's hurting. I feel it in the way he's holding me so close. With each breath, he inhales the scent of my hair, my skin. "I've missed you so much." The words are so soft, I barely hear them. I don't say anything, so he continues. "I thought so many things in my life would break me. My father dying. My mother. All the fucked-up shit I've had to endure. But nothing amounted to the pain and guilt I felt the night I lost it. The way I handled you. Spoke to you."

I lift my head off his chest and look deep into his eyes. "I forgive you, you know. I did a long time ago."

His hand brushes a loose strand of hair off my cheek. "You shouldn't have. I don't deserve your forgiveness."

"You deserve to be happy, Hayden. You deserve to live your life, free of all the demons haunting you."

"I don't know how to live that life. I'm not a good person. I don't act out of kindness. I act out of revenge. The way I've treated people...you—I don't deserve that happy life. I deserve exactly what's been coming to me."

"See, that's where you're wrong." I pull his face to mine and press my lips to his. I wait to see if he pulls away, but he does the opposite. His hands cup the side of my head, increasing the pressure of our kiss. My belly erupts with butterflies as he widens and parts my lips, pushing his tongue inside to dance around mine. There were so many nights I dreamt about having his mouth back on mine. Despite all his troubles, Hayden was my safe place. His kiss, his touch, the way he spoke to me—it all made me feel whole. Made everything else in the world right.

When that was gone, I started to question my sanity. I went home and struggled with myself. I loved him. My heart needed him. But he wasn't well. Then again, who truly is in this world? The good dreams were when he would come to me and we would make love, and his mouth would touch every single part of me. The bad ones would throw me off my axis for days—the one repeating our last night together, his hateful words and rejection. They played over and over, opening old wounds.

But being in his arms again, I know this is right. "I love you. I never stopped loving you. I need you to know that," I say through our passionate kiss.

With a quick jolt, he's up with me in his arms, carrying us down a long hallway to a bedroom. Laying me on the pristine bed that looks like it hasn't ever been slept in, he crawls on top of me.

"If there was anything missing in my life. A hole, a darkness. You were always the one to fill it. Make me feel whole." He bends down, putting his mouth over mine. We kiss and savor each emotion, feeling, this moment, as if we may not get another one, until our lungs give in and he pulls away. "Are you real? Are you going to disappear like you always do in my dreams? Am I going to wake up from this beautiful nightmare with you gone?"

My heart aches at his question. I feel the same. Having him above me. His lips on mine. The fear that this is too similar to my own dreams. I raise my hands and wrap them around his neck. "I'm real. This is real. Us. It's all real."

It takes some time for my words to fully register. For him to believe I won't fade into the back of his conscience. When they do, I watch as the fire I used to create in him lights behind his blue irises, sending a wave of sensation to my toes. "God, Katie, I've missed you." He pulls at the spaghetti strap of my summer dress, revealing my naked breast. His tongue is on my flesh, sucking my nipple hard into his mouth. "I've missed touching you, tasting you, hearing your voice, smelling every single scent you radiate." He bites down hard on my nipple, and my back bows off the mattress. "I've spent the last few months wondering if I'd ever see you again...if I ever got to touch you, if you'd taste the same—feel the same. If your cunt still knows who owns it." His fingers slide down my waist, pulling at the hem of my dress. He finds my thin panties and pushes them to the side, answering his own question. "Fuck, always so wet. You were made for me." He enters me, pushing his finger so deep, his knuckles stop him from going any further. He retracts and enters me again, then adds another finger, always knowing what I like.

"Still a little naughty one I see." He chuckles and moves to my other breast, working with his mouth and finger, until I feel the tightness in my belly. Knowing I'm on edge, he pulls his mouth off my nipple with a pop and slides down my body. Lifting my dress, he yanks on my underwear, tearing them clean off. His mouth is on me, closing around my sex while his fingers work in and out of me.

"Hayden," I purr, threading my fingers through his unruly hair. I squeeze and tug at every lick and bite. He pulls out, then slams three thick fingers back inside. It's been so long since anyone has been inside me. Before our connection in his office, three months to be exact. There's been no one since Hayden. He bites down on my clit, and I explode, white dots blasting through my frontal lobe. Before I come down, he's up and ripping off his shorts.

I wish I could freeze time to admire how beautiful he is. In every single way. He climbs back on, places the tip of his cock at my center, then looks at me, asking for approval. But he doesn't need to. I belong to him. I always have.

With a quick thrust, he pushes inside me. We moan in unison at the familiar feeling, our bodies fitting perfectly together.

"Fuck, I can't go slow with you. I want to. You deserve slow and wonderful, but I can't. I need to fuck you. And own you. And show you just how fucking bad I need you."

"Just as bad as I need you. Own me. I've always been yours," I say, knowing it will calm his worries. And it does. He pulls out and slams into me with the might of a bull. Over and over, he fucks me with fury all while I ride the waves of ecstasy.

———

The sun piercing through the windows forces me to open my eyes. I didn't mean to fall asleep. It was well past two in the morning when we both finally fell into bed, waving our white flags. I just meant to rest my eyes, then catch an uber back to Lucy's.

A wave of anxiety hits. I shouldn't have stayed. I raise my head and turn to check the time, spotting Hayden lying next to me. Eyes open. "Oh...uh...hi."

"Morning."

"I'm sorry. I didn't mean to fall asleep."

"I'm glad you did. I forgot how amazing it felt to wake up next to you."

My heart does a triple flip at this comment. I know my cheeks are starting to blush like a stupid ass schoolgirl because his mischievous smile gives it away.

"Did you want me to—?"

"Go? Never. I would keep you forever if I could." His comment is sweet yet sour all the same. A line he would say to me all the time in the past. "Shit, I'm sorry. I didn't mean to say that. I just meant...I want you to stay. I—I need you to stay."

I let the comment fade into the back of my mind and roll over so I'm facing him. "Are we okay?" I ask. What happened last night was amazing. The connection we shared, there are no words, but does that make us okay?

"I want us to be. I want so many things to be okay. I want these past few months to never have happened. I want a redo with you. With my brothers. With Trevor."

"And your dad?" I ask, knowing today is the day—the second anniversary of Eric's death.

"I just want to be at peace with him. He was who he was. Some of us chose to love him for that, and some didn't. I was supposed to shelter Camden from all the hate, and I was the one leading the parade right to our front door."

"Are you and Trevor okay?" I have to ask. Lucy was only able to give me bits and pieces of their throw-down. I know Hayden felt defeated after their argument. He spent months with this theory making him sick only to find out the truth is beyond what he could imagine.

"I just don't know what to do with that information. I don't know if I should tell Nixon. He has the right to know. He almost looked disappointed when I'd confirmed Trevor wasn't his father. As if I took something from him. Now, to bring up all those old emotions, would I be doing more harm than good?"

If anyone is deserving of love more than Hayden, it's Nix. And I have to agree. What good would it do to let him know a deadbeat con artist was his real father?

Hayden reaches for my hand, pulling it to his heart. "Will you come with me today...with us to the cemetery and the party afterwards?"

I give him a look that he knows well. The look I gave

in the past when he needed reassurance.

"I'll be right next to you the entire way."

EIGHT

H A Y D E N

"CRAZY, IT'S BEEN TWO YEARS. SOMETIMES IT feels like yesterday," Nixon says, handing Erica a rose and encouraging her to lay it on the headstone. Rowan sniffles and smiles at Nixon as she squeezes his arm for support.

I barely remember burying him.

I remember the weather, though.

It was sunny, not a cloud in the sky. I'm sure he had a hissy fit up there bossing everyone around on how he wanted his burial to turn out. He never took shit from anyone. Except maybe Trevor. There was a story floating around that Trevor broke Dad's nose over him interfering with him and Lucy. Trevor nor Lucy have confirmed our suspicions, but we all think my dad, for the first time ever, got his ass kicked.

"Do you think he watches over us? Like how they all say dead people do when they die?" The five of us look at Brock, not sure if he's fucking with us or not. "*What?* Just curious. I've been watching those medium shows at school where they talk to the dead and they're all haunted by their relatives and shit." He shrugs his shoulders and tosses his flowers.

If he were, I wonder what he would say? Would he be proud of his sons? Would he approve of Nixon's dedication to his daughter? Would he tell me he's proud of how I'm handling Four Fathers? Would he still coddle Camden and quiz him night after night like I do now on his knowledge of politics and foreign trade?

Would he ever tell us he was glad he had four sons?

"I think he did the best he could with us. He had his own demons—we all do. I think, in the end, he went down exactly how he would have wanted to—swinging." Camden's statement is truer than any of us could have put into our own words. He throws his flower onto the grave and wraps his arms around Rowan, who's silently weeping.

I debate over what I would say to my father if he were standing in front of me today. At one point, I would have told him how much I hated him—despised him for how he made me feel. The way he always made sure he knew he had control over us all. But today, standing here, the sun beating down on me, staring at his headstone, I would say thank you. For showing me how to survive. To thrive when times are tough. And to learn to fight through the weak moments knowing there's a reward in strength. I would say: here's to letting go.

Katie's hand wraps around mine as I lift my other hand and toss my flower onto his grave.

"Now that that's out of the way, shall we celebrate the day, Eric Pearson style, with a pool party?" Brock says, and with sadness etched behind everyone's smile, we head to the one place where it all started to celebrate where it all came to an end.

———

Ethan jumps in the pool with Brock on his tail. Rowan squeals as she gets splashed and starts yelling profanities for getting Erica wet. I watch as Nixon dives into the pool to avenge his girl and the three of them wrestle until Ethan waves the white flag.

I look over to see Trevor still manhandling the grill laughing. Lucy, cradling a sleeping Eva, is on his ass for buying lobster tails. Don't know what the fuck that's all about, but she sure seems pissed. I turn over to see my girl sitting next to me, looking content and happy.

My girl.

Is she my girl?

We fucked and talked and fucked 'til the sun came up. We talked about our past, and issues I should have put on the table months ago. I told her things I should have told her instead of letting her walk out of my house months ago. That I fucking loved her. That she was my rock. That she was everything to me the second I saw her walk through those hospital doors. And even though she told me the same, there was no mention of the future.

The deja vu created a whirlwind of anxiety inside me. Me asking her to stay again, and even though she should leave, she'll stay. What if the same shit happens? She doesn't deserve that. But I don't know that I can let her leave again.

"Is it weird being back here?" Katie asks, breaking into my thoughts.

"Yes and no. Is it weird knowing they haven't torn down the fucking psychopath's personal cemetery next door? Yes. But here? No matter what bad happened, good things happened too. It will always be home."

"Is that why you haven't sold it yet?"

I shrug. "Maybe. Now that I'm thinking with a clearer head..." I turn to her and wink, "maybe it's time to let it go. Sell. Move on. Nixon has mentioned a few ideas for the land. Maybe I'll just give it over to him."

She squeezes my hand and brings her eyes back to the pool. Everyone does seem happy. Content. Maybe dear old dad *is* looking down on us. I hear the door chimes ringing through the outdoor speakers, indicating someone's at the front door.

"I'll be right back," I tell Katie, kissing the top of her hand and making my way through the house. Opening the door, I'm met with a face I'd never thought I'd see.

"Well, well…looks like there's a party going on and your dear old step daddy wasn't invited."

Jameson Vincent.

The same guy from the photo, even though he looks like he's been through a few wars and back.

"What the fuck do you want, asshole?"

"Wow, is that any way to talk to family?"

I take a menacing step toward him. There's something about his blank stare that fucking screams Nixon, and it's unsettling. "You ain't family to shit. Get off my fucking property before I shoot you for trespassing."

I go to slam the door, but he puts his foot in the way to stop it. "I don't think so, sonny. We're not done talkin'."

I look down at his foot, willing my fiery gaze to set his shoe on fire. "We're done. Remove your foot or lose it."

"Not before I get paid."

He's insane if he thinks he's getting another dime from us. I'll tell Nixon if I need to before I give him another cent. "Good luck. Payday's over for you, asshole." I kick his foot out of the door and begin to shut it just as his words stifle through the crack.

"Oh, I think payday is right now." He lifts his phone to the closed window as a video plays on his screen.

The color fades from my face.

What the fuck?

"That's right. Now, open up and offer me a burger, why don'tcha?"

"Where the fuck did you get this?"

"Well, I was going to visit my nephew. You see, he got sloppy with putting my money into my account, and just as I pull up, who do I see in a little pink car? A boy with Daddy's eyes."

I stand there in shock, unsure what to do. I can't bear to watch the video any longer, so I give in and open the door. I don't spit another word, and he follows me through the house to the back. I throw my hand out, telling that motherfucker to hold back as I open the door and yell for my brothers and Trevor to get the fuck in the kitchen.

Just as Trevor walks through the sliding glass doors, his eyes land on Jameson. "What the fuck are you doing here?" he barks, ready to fight. I throw my hand out to stop him.

"We have a problem," I say.

"No, we don't," Trevor bites out, turning to Jameson.

"We do. He has a video of Nixon killing Jaxson Wheeler."

NINE

H A Y D E N

"WE KILL HIM."

"No." Trevor steps forward, putting a stop to Brock's suggestion. Jameson is long gone and the four of us and Trevor are standing in the kitchen, leaving the girls outside, so they don't catch wind of what's happening.

"Why the fuck not? No one would miss him."

"Because killing is not the answer," Trevor replies.

"But it's okay for fucking Nixon to just go offing people?"

"Shut the fuck up, Brock," I snap.

Brock steps forward, challenging me. "Fuckin' make me, bro." I eliminate the space between us. I'm done with his bullshit attitude. Our chests bump, and Brock raises his closed fists. My reaction time is quicker, and my two hands are up, shoving him back. "Fuck you, Hay. You think just 'cause you're the oldest you control us all? Fuck you."

I shove him again, and his back hits the counter. "Oh, you think I enjoy the fucking role Dad put me in? Having to grow the fuck up and babysit *you* three?" I regret the words the second they leave my mouth. I immediately turn to Camden. "I didn't mean that." He nods, hopefully in understanding. Turning back to Brock, I say, "I didn't ask for any of this either. You wanna go live free, have at it. I'm fucking done trying to keep you out of trouble."

Brock scoffs. "Trouble? You fucking joking me here? Coming from the guy who's spent the last three months being nothing but trouble. Big, bad Hayden Pearson. So untouchable. You're probably the most fucked up out of us all. But then again, our bother here might take the cake for *murdering* some—"

I tackle him.

We both fall to the ground and my arm cocks back, punching him square in the jaw. He manages a swift punch to my ribs. I lose my grip, and he flips me, raising his fist and getting a good shot to my nose. Before I have a chance at another swing, Trevor rips him off me.

I'm off the ground and ready for round two, but he has a solid grip on my shoulders, restraining me. I throw my shoulders back. "Get the fuck off me," I snap, and wipe the blood dripping from my nose. Trevor obeys, releasing me.

"You need to chill out," Nixon says, and I turn to him and explode.

"Were you ever going to tell us? Me? Anyone? You just kill someone and go on your merry fucking way?"

He shrugs, as if I asked him what he wants on his pizza and he doesn't care. "He had to die. He was going to hurt Lucy again. I couldn't risk him coming for Rowan... for Erica. I did what none of you would have been able to do. So shut the fuck up and get the hell over it."

I drag my hands over my scalp and pull so hard, I fear tearing my hair out. "Yeah, so you call the fucking cops! He has a video of you. Do you understand what that means? You could go to jail. He fucking has a VIDEO!" I yell. I squeeze my eyes tightly shut, but when I reopen them, Nixon is no longer in front of me. I turn just in time to see the sliding glass door slam shut and watch Nixon tread over to a concerned looking Rowan.

"He won't tell her. Don't worry."

I look at Camden, then back to Nixon, who's now cradling Erica in his arms. "What?"

"He won't tell Rowan about her dad. It would kill her. He wouldn't do anything to hurt her."

I shake my head. Hurting Rowan's feelings is the last thing on my fucking mind right now. I have to figure out how to fix this. I can't let my brother go to jail.

All these years, and he kept this secret to himself.

"We need to get those videos," I say to the room.

"Yeah, but to get them, we have to pay. A lot," Camden

says. Jameson demanded five hundred thousand dollars. Technically, that's pocket change for us, but he demanded that once a month to keep quiet or he sends the video to the cops. He gave us twenty-four hours to decide where the fate of our brother's future lies and left with a smile on his face knowing he had us. He also made sure we knew he had a copy if we tried right then and there to take him out.

"Even if we pay, we have no idea what he'll do with the video. We have no idea how many copies he's made." He could have more than the two he claims.

"What do you need me to do?" Camden asks, and I turn my eyes on him.

"Nothing. You stay the fuck out of this. I don't want you near this. You have too much to lose. I'll handle it." There is no way I'm going to allow him to fuck up his future.

"I agree with Hayden on this one," Brock chimes in. "He and I will handle this."

I turn to my brother. "No, you won't do shit either. You will stay just as far away from this as Cam."

Brock throws his hands up. "Seriously? Can you never not have complete control? You know what? Fuck it. You win. I'm outta here." He storms out through the front door, and minutes later, we hear him peeling out of the driveway.

No one speaks until the silent tension is broken by the sliding glass door opening and Lucy appearing through it. "Everything okay in here?" Trevor walks up to her and pulls her into his chest.

No, everything is not fucking okay.

We're fucked.

There's no other way around it.

———

The second the door to my condo shuts, I'm on her. "I need to fuck you," I tell her, no apology in my tone. I need to be inside her and fuck her hard and ruthless. I grab her shoulders and bring her against the door. Her eyes light up. She always loved it rough. I'm pleased to see she still does. I rip the front of her bathing suit cover-up off without a care and pull at the strap to her top, then bottoms, until she's completely naked before me. "How is it possible that you get more and more perfect," I praise her, squeezing her tit in my hand.

"It's tough, but I seem to manage," she laughs, ending on a moan when I pinch her nipple between my fingers. "Hayden..."

The sound of my name off her lips is like heaven. I never thought I would have her back in my life.

"Yeah, baby?" I take my knee and widen her legs, so I can get to where I crave to be. "You wet for me already?" I already know she is. I just want her to admit how aroused she gets for me.

"Soaked," she purrs, making my dick hard as stone. My hands find her pussy, and just as I thought, she's drenched.

"Naughty girl. I'm gonna have some fun with this

pussy." She can't even hide the excitement from my comment. My dick jolts at the mental image of all the ways I plan on taking her. I spread her lips open and shove two fingers inside her. Her moans become muffled when I slam my mouth on hers.

Thrust.

Thrust.

Thrust.

I pump my fingers deep inside, fucking her with my hand, until I feel her death squeeze around me. "Jesus," I grunt, ripping my fingers out. I tear my board shorts off. "Turn around," I growl, then grab her waist, whipping her around. Her hands go up against the door and I spread her legs wide for me.

"This ass is mine. Only mine," I state.

My mind is so fogged over with lust, the urge to take and control her. I take my palm and slap it across her pale skin. She jumps at the assault, but there's no hiding the small moan that follows. "You're mine. Do you hear me?"

She takes too long to answer, so I swipe my open palm across her now pink cheek.

"Yes, I'm yours." God, she's so fucking sexy. Her voice, low and dripping with need.

"Good." I take my raging hard cock and shove it in her from behind. I fuck her and fuck her and fuck her until a deep growl travels up my throat. My balls tighten and my orgasm shoots through me, almost knocking me out.

It doesn't go unnoticed that I just came inside her. It's not the first time, and fuck if it will be the last. I'm feeling so goddamn territorial over her, I'm tempted to smear my cum all over her so everyone knows who she belongs to. The thought alone has me hard again already and pumping inside her.

"Another round? I must be a lucky girl," she teases.

"Oh, baby, hope you like it here, because I'm gonna fuck you so long and hard, you won't be able to walk— just to make sure you can never leave."

———

"You wanna talk about it?"

It's two in the morning and we're finally falling into bed, completely spent and sated. I followed Brock's lead and got the fuck outta that house. I told everyone to sit tight and I'd reach out first thing. Trevor made me promise not to do anything irrational. I agreed, knowing I was lying. He doesn't get to make the decisions for this family. This is my burden to bear.

"I can't right now. I don't want to keep anything from you, but it's just some family shit I gotta take care of." She looks concerned, so I ease her worries. "Don't worry, I've let all the Trevor bullshit go—something I should have done a long time ago."

She cuddles up closer to me, and I hold her tight in my arms.

"Hayden, can I ask you a question?"

"Anything, beautiful." I kiss the top of her head.

"Do you think you'll ever sell the house?"

"Why, you lookin' to buy it?" I tease, giving her body a playful shake.

"No, just curious. Just wonder why you still hold onto it. If you'll stay here once Cam goes off to college."

"I figured we'll just live here until Cam leaves, then we can look for a place of our own closer to the beach."

"Wait..." Katie pulls from my embrace and sits up. "Hayden, I'm not staying."

Confusion strikes. I shake my head. "What do you mean you're not staying? Of course you are. You said you're mine."

"I am, but that doesn't mean—"

Those eyes. She's always been one to reveal so much just by looking at her. She's gonna leave again. Just like before. Why would I think she would want to stay and be with a fuck up like me?

I sit up. "The fuck it doesn't," I snap and toss my legs out from under the sheet.

"Hayden...just...let's talk about this."

"No, fuck that. I thought we were good. I love you. I know you fucking love me. So what's there to talk about?"

"History repeating itself."

It's as if she slapped me. Her words sting.

"Please understand where I'm coming from. I love you, but—"

"Bullshit you do!" I yell and climb out of bed.

"What? How can you even question that?" she cries.

"Are you for real right now? You just told me you have no intentions of being with me." Storming over to my dresser, I rip open the top drawer and grab a pair of boxers.

"No, I said I wasn't staying. That's different."

"Well, good, thanks for letting me in on your plans." I grab a t-shirt and throw it over my head. "Next time you're in town, make sure to give me a heads up. I love a good weekend fuck."

My words cut her even deeper.

"Don't do this again."

"Do what? Make sure I know next time I'm just a fuck to you?"

"No, try to degrade what we have."

"We have?" I bite back. "What we have is you toying me along, making me think I had you back and then informing me I had it all wrong."

"Hayden, I never expected this, and when it all happened, it happened so fast...just like before. I need to be guarded about my decisions this time."

That jolts me.

I pause, my voice eerily calm. "You have to be guarded around me?"

"That's not what I said."

"Is this because of that night? You're afraid I'd what? Hurt you or some shit?"

"No, Hayden—"

"Fuck it, I don't need any more details. I get it."

"Hayden, please!" she pleads for me to listen, but I can't. I jam my legs into a pair of jeans and walk out of my bedroom.

"Hayden!" she calls my name again, with no response. I grab my phone off the counter and notice a text from a random number.

1-652-555-6552: Meet me at 1421 Timber Drive. Bring my money.

I click open an attachment, and my stomach turns as the video begins to play. Bile rises up my throat as I watch Nixon wrap a noose around Jax Wheeler's neck.

Random images of Nixon as a happy child flash through my mind. Him smiling. Playing with us older brothers. Today holding Erica.

He doesn't deserve this.

He deserves a happy life.

The feeling that resonates inside me is purpose. Like a calm before the storm. I know what I need to do.

I walk back to my bedroom and dig through my closet. I reach what I'm looking for and pull out the wooden box. I take a quick glance at my mother's initials before opening the box.

"What are you doing?"

I ignore Katie's question, pull out the gun, and stuff it in the back of my jeans.

"Jesus, Hayden, what are you doing!"

I stand and walk out. Katie is fast on my heels. "Hayden, you're scaring me. I'm calling Trevor!"

I make it to the door before turning to her. "Good. At least you're finally being honest with me. Have a safe flight home." Opening the door, I walk out, slamming it behind me.

TEN ——————

H A Y D E N

I PULL UP TO THE ADDRESS JAMESON TEXTED ME, but there's not a light on in the run-down house. I expected it to be nicer considering all the money he's scammed from Trevor the past eight years.

I get out of my car and walk up the pathway to the front door. The grass is a foot tall with wild flowers along the walkway. I wonder if he's been here the whole time. Knowing Wyatt Brandon has been dicking me over for months, I wonder if he even bothered looking for him.

I take a closed fist to the door and bang three times, letting him know I'm here. The weight of the gun feels like a million pounds in the back of my jeans. My phone continued to ring the whole way over her with Katie's number popping up, so I shut it off. I need to focus. I can't think about the pain that will soon settle in knowing she'll be gone again.

I need to focus on my family. My brothers.

This is what family does for one another.

They sacrifice.

My impatience is growing, so I bang again, this time even harder. The door creaks and opens. "The fuck?" I push it the rest of the way and walk in. My eyes need to adjust to the darkness. Even with the sun beginning to pop through, it's hard to see. "Where the fuck are you, Vincent? Let's get this over with."

I walk a little farther into the house, but still, nothing. If he's not even here, I'm going to fucking lose my shit. I flip on a light switch, but nothing happens. The place almost looks like it's been ransacked.

My intuition is starting to tell me this is a bad idea. I should come back at night. How am I going to shoot a man in daylight? How am I going to kill a man who isn't even fucking here? "Jameson!" I call out again, but nothing. "Fuck!" I kick a box on the floor and a red blinking light appears. I bend down to investigate, realizing it's a recorder.

He was going to record us.

I click stop and rewind it to the start.

"What took you so long—?"

Oomph... "What the fuck, asshole!"

"Well, that's no way to talk to your son, is it?"

Nixon.

"You should learn some manners on how to treat your elders—"

Oomph... "Goddammit, boy!"

"Get up. We're takin' a trip."

"I ain't goin' nowhere. Got plans with your other psycho brother—"

Oomph... "Jesus, put that bat down."

"Get up. I'm not going to ask you again."

"Where the fuck we goin'?"

"To a favorite place of mine. With a postcard view."

Sounds of shuffling and the slamming of the door is the last thing I hear before the recording turns to static. Fucking Nixon. What has he done? I listen to the tape once more, trying to figure out where he's taking him.

With a postcard view.

"Think, fucking think..."

Postcard...

The cottage house on the beach Dad bought for him and Rowan. Nixon always laughed at how cute Rowan thought it was and joked about how it had a postcard view.

Fuck!

I run out the door and speed away, hoping I'm not too late.

━━━━

I pull up to the house, and sure enough, Nixon's car is parked in the driveway. I jump out and run to the front door, bursting through it. "Nixon!" I yell his name, but I don't have to look far to spot him—or Jameson. "Nixon, don't," I say, my eyes glued to the gun he has pointed at Jameson's head, who's tied to a chair.

"Go home, Hayden. This doesn't involve you."

"Yes, it does, man. You're my brother. I told you to let me handle this." I take a slow step closer, not wanting to set him off.

"He was going to ruin Rowan's life. If she found out what I did, she wouldn't be able to handle it. She'd leave me."

I take another step. "No, she wouldn't. She loves you." I look at Jameson to evaluate the condition he's in. He's bleeding from his mouth and nose, one eye is swollen shut, and he smells like a bucket of piss.

"She wouldn't if she found out what I did. He was too dangerous to leave alive. I couldn't put her at risk. He needed to die."

Jameson is wiggling from side to side, trying to loosen his binds. I'm worried he's going to make a move forward and cause Nixon to accidently pull the trigger.

One more step closer. "Nixon, give me the gun. This isn't the answer. Please. Let me handle this."

He turns to me. "Oh, it's not? And what do you think the answer is? Cam called me. Said he spoke to a hysterical Katie. Seems you took off with a gun yourself. What did *you* plan on doing with it, brother?"

Fuck.

"Exactly. Don't tell me this isn't the right thing. We both know he needs to die. It's the only way we go on." He brings his focus back to Jameson.

"Nixon," I plead.

"Go home, Hayden. Eric entrusted in you to do great things. I was the fuck up. He knew it. We all know it. I'm not right. I never will be."

"Nixon, that's not true. Who gives a shit what Dad wanted? It's not about him anymore. It's about us. And us living our own lives now. Rowan needs you. Erica needs you. I need you. I love you, man."

My last comment jerks him. He turns to me just as

Jameson leaps from the chair and tackles Nixon to the ground, trying to wrestle the gun from his hands. I pull the gun from the back of my jeans and aim at the ground. They're moving around too fast, I can't get a good shot. My finger compresses on the trigger, but I'm too afraid I'll hit Nixon. My heart races and my palms become slick with sweat. I need to do something fast.

Fuck!

I race over to help Nixon when the gun goes off, the sound echoing throughout the small cottage.

Nixon's eyes widen. "Hayden," Nixon says my name. His voice seems off. Distant almost.

Time slows.

I can't pull my eyes away from Nixon's.

They scream fear.

A sudden burning sensation in my gut causes me to look down. Blood expands from my stomach, a red dot growing like an ink stain. Time speeds up when I bring my hands to my abdomen. Red covers my palms.

"Hayden!" Nixon barks, coming toward me, but he's too late. I collapse to the ground, no longer able to hold myself up. The pain is excruciating. Like a ball of fire just exploded inside my stomach. Nixon leans over me, putting his hands to my wound to stop the bleeding. "Hayden, fuck. Don't die, please, FUCK!"

There's more commotion. The door is open. More voices.

Trevor.

"Call 9-1-1!"

Nixon is gone from my vision, replaced by Trevor. "Stay with us, son. You're going to be okay." I take solace in his words. I'm suddenly tired, so I close my eyes. "Stay awake. Hayden, you have to keep your eyes open, okay?" I want to. I'm trying to, but I'm so fucking tired. My arm feels like it weighs a million pounds, but I manage to lift it and wrap my fingers around Trevor's wrist while his are over my open wound.

"I'm sorry," I croak, the words hard to speak. I start

to choke. I'm struggling to get air into my lungs.

"Don't you do that. Don't you fucking do that!" he yells at me.

"I'm sorry," I repeat, because I am. For so many things. If there is one thing I want them to know, it's that I'm sorry for how I've treated them all. The hateful way I've acted with Trevor. My failed attempt at being a guardian to Camden. Maybe if I had been a better brother to Nixon, he wouldn't be as fucked up. Maybe if I just accepted Brock for who he is, we wouldn't have grown apart the last couple years.

Suddenly, my other brothers are beside me. "Shut up, bro. You're not dying." Brock.

"Yeah, I need you to sign off on my college shit. Gonna need you to live, okay, man?" Camden. I can hear it in his voice. He's crying.

The faint sounds of sirens ring out in the background. I'm hoping it's okay now to close my eyes, so I do. The yelling and cries are mumbling together.

I'm just so tired.

Black.

ELEVEN ———

K A T I E

I BARREL THROUGH THE DOORS OF THE ER AND PUSH past a crowd standing in front of the nurse's station. "Excuse me, a man was brought in. Gun shot. Hayd—"

"Katie."

I whip to my left to see Camden.

"Where is he?"

He walks up to me and takes my hand. "He's in surgery," he says and walks me to the sitting area, where I spot Brock and Nixon. Oh god. Nixon is covered in blood.

"Surgery? Why surgery? What happened?" I look to each brother. No one responds. "What the fuck happened!" I scream in hysterics. I was with Lucy when we got the call. Trevor told her Hayden had been shot.

"Keep your voice down," Nixon finally speaks up.

"Then talk to me. Someone, please." I start to cry again.

Brock stands and storms off. I look to Camden for some answers, then Nixon. "What are you hiding?" Nixon looks away. "Nixon, what are you—?"

"Nixon?" Trevor's voice cuts in. I turn to him, and the uniformed gentleman standing with him. "Sorry, but this officer needs to ask you a few questions."

Nixon looks at Trevor, and I swear they exchange a silent message.

"Yeah, whatever."

"Mr. Pearson, my name is Dexter Forbes. I'm with the Tampa Bay P.D. Would you mind giving me a rundown of what happened this morning?"

"My brother and I went to meet up at my cottage house off Lincoln Bay. He said he had gotten in a fight with his girlfriend and needed to talk. We walked in on an intruder trying to rob the place. He had a gun. I tackled him. While we were wrestling, the gun went off. My brother was shot."

"*Oh god.*" I cover my mouth. My stomach turns, and I keel over, struggling to get air into my lungs.

"Mr. Pearson, did you recognize the intruder? Do you know what happened to him?"

"No. I ran to my brother, and he got away. It all happened so fast, I didn't pay much attention to him or get a good look."

"Would you know or have any reason for someone to target the house? Maybe a—"

"That's enough. His brother is fighting for his life right now. This all can wait," Trevor breaks in, stopping any further questioning.

The officer nods. "I understand. My thoughts are with you all. If you think of anything else, please give us a call. We have patrols searching the area. We'll let you know any updates." He hands Nixon a business card and leaves.

His brother is fighting for his life.

I can't breathe.

"Wh—Where did he get shot?" Please say in the arm or leg.

Nixon's face is sullen as he responds. "The stomach."

"No," I gasp, losing my strength. My legs give out, and I collapse. Trevor is on me, lifting me up just before I hit the floor. "Is...is he alive?" I don't know how I have the courage to ask a question I don't want the answer to.

"He was when they brought him in," Camden says grimly.

No. He can't die.

The sullen look Camden holds tells me he can't guarantee he won't.

———

"Tell me, or I'm gonna rip your cheap ass hair extensions out and shove them up your ass!" I scream.

A set of hands wrap around me, pulling me away from the nurse's station. "Let me go! I need an update!

They need to give us a fucking UPDATE!" Camden doesn't let me go until we're seated back in the waiting room from hell. We've been here almost six hours, and all we've been told is Hayden is still in surgery. That was three hours ago. We don't know if he's alive. If he's dead. *Oh god.* I begin to sob again. I can't look at Nixon. He has yet to change out of his soiled shirt.

"It's going to be okay." Camden tries to comfort me, but he doesn't know that. Such a bullshit thing people say.

"You don't know that."

"No, but I do know Hayden is a fighter." He squeezes my hand, his fancy watch glittering under the dull halogen lights above us. For a moment, I grow fixated on the way the second-hand tick, tick, ticks around in a circle. His thumb taps the back of my hand in tandem with the seconds, and it serves to calm me some.

"Why do you love watches so much?" I ask abruptly—anything to drive my mind from what's going on in surgery.

Camden's features grow stormy. The always smiling, happy young man mask he wears is gone. He blinks several times before saying, "I just do."

A whine of emotion escapes me. He sounds so much like Hayden, it hurts. "Oh God."

"Hey," he says softly, returning to his normal demeanor. "Big, bad, and wild, remember? He wouldn't take off on us this easily."

The nickname his brothers gave him when they were younger sparks so many memories, starting with our second encounter.

"There you go again," I say to him. He seems to keep losing himself in his thoughts.

"Go where?" he asks.

"In your head. Wanna talk about it?" I doubt he wants to confess all his problems to a stranger, but I feel far from that to him. It's weird. I know I've only known him for a short time, but it feels like I've known him forever.

"That's fine. How about I just do what someone did for me once. It was a real life-saver for me."

"*Oh? And what was that?*" he asks.

I don't even think he realizes our hands are still connected. I lift them and say, "This." He stares intently at our joined hands. I wonder if he can feel the small buzz between us. I follow suit and stare out at the water, being okay with the silence.

"Katie?"

"*Yeah?*" *I turn to give him my attention.*

"*Do you believe in fate? Things in life that are meant to happen?*"

I wonder what sparks this question. Is it everything that has happened in his life? Is it meeting me? Oh god, don't be silly, Katie. He barely knows you. "*I do,*" *I answer him honestly.*

"*Do you believe in guardian angels?*"

I laugh, then shift my entire body, giving him my full attention. "Okay, you got me. What's with the random questions?"

He's back to staring at the water. He takes so long to respond, I almost feel like he doesn't plan to. Then, he turns to me. It's the first time I've ever seen him smile and it does something to me. "Good. Because I have a feeling one day soon, you're gonna fall in love with me. I'm irresistible, so it won't be hard. And when you do, I'm going to ask you to stay and live out the rest of our days together just like they do in those cheesy, but oh so heartwarming fairytales."

Three months later, I called and asked for a leave of absence from my job, had my brother pack up most of my necessities and ship them to me, and locked in a six-month sub-lease on my apartment. It took me under a week to fall madly in love with Hayden Pearson. He always guilted me, saying I took so long to fall in love with him since he claimed he fell in love with me that day by the pool.

"He's going to leave me. He's going to leave me." I cry into Cam's shoulder at the thought of Hayden never giving me the chance to prove to him how much I love him. Fate didn't bring us together, not once, but twice, to have him leave me.

"Stop, have faith in him." He holds me to him. "You know, he never once stopped loving you. He was so hard on himself for what happened between you two. I think it's why he's been so cold the past few months. He never showed his feelings about what happened, but it was apparent he was hurting. He never got personal with me, but one time, he was pretty drunk having a fucked-up talk about my dad and you were brought up." He goes into the memory.

"Do you think Dad would have done what he did, knowing it was going to get his head blown off?"

Hayden starts laughing and chugs the rest of his beer. "Damn, dude, a little morbid, don't you think?"

"How so? It's what happened, isn't it? He had it all and lost everything for her. I just don't know what's so great you'd risk losing your whole life."

Hayden gets quiet.

"What? Would you ever sacrifice your life for someone?"

"Katie. I would for Katie."

"He didn't say anything else after that. He shut down. But the little glimpse of himself he gave me...I guess it told me what I already knew. He loves you like no other."

I've soaked his shirt. My tears are pouring from my eyes. I can't breathe. "I love him so much. He accused me of not. If he dies, he's going to die thinking I didn't love him."

"Shhh..." He pats my back. "Let's not get dramatic. Hayden is probably back there laughing at us all, eating green Jell-O. Chin up, kid."

I pull my head away and give him a crazy look for calling me kid. "You know I'm like ten years older than you, right?"

"Yeah, but I'm what you call an old soul. One day, when I'm sitting in my seat in the oval office, you'll remember this moment and think, man, that Camden Pearson was a wise man."

I didn't think it was possible at a time like this, but I smile. "Thank you."

He shrugs, acting calm for us both. As if his own brother isn't fighting for his life. The doors to the emergency room open and we both look to see Brock storm in.

"Any news?" he asks as he approaches us.

"Nothing. Not since the last time I texted. Is it done?" Camden asks.

Brock nods. "It's done."

———

We're going on nine hours.

Nine of the longest hours of my life.

Everyone is here. Lucy has Eva sleeping in her arms. Trevor, Brock, and Camden. Nixon left to take Rowan and Erica home to get Erica to bed, but has long since returned, changed and showered. Every once in a while, I glance over at Trevor. He's in bad shape. Even Lucy's calming touch isn't settling him. I haven't been around him to witness his outbursts, but now, I get it. He's taking this very hard.

I move my attention to Brock and Camden, who are in a heated conversation in the corner. Something is going on with those two. I've asked a billion times what the real story is. I know they're lying. Everyone is. Even Trevor. I can't take it any longer. I jump up and head toward them. I'm going to force them to tell me what really happened.

"Just answer my fucking question. Did anyone see you?" Camden spits out to Brock, who shakes his head.

"Who saw what?" I ask, and they both jump. "Something's up. I'm not dumb. Tell me what really happened. I don't believe for a second it was an—"

"Pearson family?"

I snap my attention to the doctor. He's pulling off his hair cap and threading his fingers through his hair. He looks tired. Defeated.

No...

Everyone rushes to him, question after question being thrown at him.

Is he alive?

How did the surgery go?

Can we see him?

I want the same answers, but my legs refuse to move. I can't hear him say those words. I can't hear them explain he did what he could and he's sorry for our loss.

"Katie." I hear my name being called. I snap out of it to see Cam calling me over. I numbly walk over to hear the doctor begin speaking.

"The surgery went as well as could be expected. He lost a lot of blood. The bullet penetrated the abdomen. It didn't puncture any internal organs surprisingly. He's very lucky to be alive." *He's alive. He's alive.* "We have him stable at the moment, but the next twenty-four to seventy-two hours will really determine."

"Can we see him?" Trevor asks.

The doctor hesitates before responding. "Yes, but for

a short time. I will warn you, we had to put him into an induced coma. It's just a precaution. To let his body heal."

Everyone asks to go in first. "Please, only one or two at the moment. And just family at this time."

Nixon reaches out and grabs my hand, pulling me forward. "She's his fiancée." My eyes widen. I look to Cam and Brock. They should go first.

Cam rests his hand on my shoulder. "It's okay. He needs you more than us right now." With a silent thanks, I continue to hold Nixon's hand and follow the doctor through the wide hospital doors.

———

There's never any preparation on how to handle seeing someone you love laying in a hospital bed, connected by tubes and monitors. He doesn't look like himself. Pale, swollen. The doctor warned us before entering his room. The liquid they're pumping him with is causing him to look bloated. Another precaution they're taking. I hear a sound next to me, and realize

Nixon's grinding his teeth.

"Oh, Nixon." I wrap my arms around him.

"This is all my fault. I did this."

"No, you didn't. You didn't shoot him."

"I might as well have." His shoulders tense as I try to offer him comfort. I don't think I've ever seen Nixon show such emotion before. I can't help feeling overwhelmed by his grief and anger. I begin to cry on him and he lets me.

We stay like that for some time, until Nixon finally breaks away from my hold. "I can't be in here. I...I'm gonna give you a moment." And he's gone.

The room is eerily quiet aside from the beeping of the machine and ventilator. I pull a chair up to his bedside and sit. He's so still, the rise and fall of his chest the only movement. His hand is cold when I touch it. I'm afraid to do anything else, worried I'll hurt him.

"You know when I told you it took me seven days to fall in love with you? All the shit you gave me, because you knew right off the bat I was your angel sent to save you from yourself? Well...I lied. I fell in love with you the day you slipped your hand through mine. I felt it. The buzz between us. My heart grew that day because it needed more room for all the love I felt. You asked me if I believed in fate. I said yes, but I never truly told you why." I wipe a tear from my cheek. "You always told me I saved you. But truthfully, you saved me first. My life before you, it was so lonely. I'd been falling into my own hole of depression. I never shared because I didn't want to burden you when you were already dealing with so much. I struggled with finding purpose for myself. When Lucy left, she took any happiness and peace with her. She was my best friend. And when she left, I was alone.

"I've never told anyone this, but I spent a few weeks in a facility. I told Lucy I was away on a work trip, but I checked myself in. I had a rough night and tried to commit suicide. I failed, thankfully, and the next day, I checked myself in to a clinic. I needed help in a bad way, but I didn't want the solution to be death. A few days after I returned home was when I got the call about Lucy. I rushed to Florida, and then...I met you. It was as if you were *my* angel. You gave *me* purpose. You gave me something I feared I would never experience—a love so profound, there's no actual word to describe it."

I have to stop to catch my breath. The tears are making it hard to see.

"When I left you, it almost killed me again. I wanted nothing more than to help you. See you through your darkness just like you secretly did mine. I couldn't see life without you in it, but I didn't know if I was helping you or hurting you. So, I stayed away." My cries turn into sobs. "I stayed away because I wanted you to be better. But neither of us was better. Being back here made me realize that. We are who we are. But our love is what will always guide us. I'm sorry I left. I should have stayed. I shouldn't have let you push me away. And now, now you may leave me, and I won't be able to survive that. I can't have you leave me. Our story isn't done yet. Please, please don't leave me."

I sob, holding his hand, begging him to heal and come back to me. Tell me he forgives me. That he loves me. That we're going to be okay. But he does none of the above. He just lays there, as if he's sleeping, but in reality, he's fighting for his life.

TWELVE———

H A Y D E N

I HEAR THEM ALL.

Each one that comes into my room.

I hear them.

It's a surreal feeling. I want to be able to talk back, and in my mind, I do, but they don't respond to anything I say. I beg Katie to stay, but my pleas go unheard. Soon, her voice is distant, and then she's gone.

Time doesn't exist where I'm at. I don't know how long it's been. I wonder when Katie will come back and talk to me. I have so much to say back. Camden's voice brings me back to the surface. His voice sounds strange. He sounds upset, and I'm not sure why. I feel fine. I'll be fine.

"I've got plans. Just you wait. Big office. Big moves. You

show off with running Four Fathers, just wait 'til it's my turn to show off. You'll all be begging for a piece of the youngest Pearson."

I never expected anything less, little brother.

"I know you doubt yourself. But you've been a great big brother."

I haven't been. I should have been better for you.

"...and I wouldn't have our life any other way. Maybe not Dad's head blown off," he chuckles.

I laugh with him. But then he's not laughing anymore. Why is he crying? Don't cry for me, Cam. I'm not worth it.

———

With every voice I hear, I begin to wonder if I died. Am I stuck in an afterlife? Why can I hear them, but they can't hear me? Everyone sounds so sad.

"You didn't deserve this. The hardships your father put you through."

Trevor.

"I know you have been so angry with me. You've had a hard life. But I never wanted anything but the best for you. All your brothers. I love you like you're my own. That's never changed."

Why is he getting so upset? He sounds like he's crying. His voice fades in and out until I no longer hear him. He must be gone. Where is everyone going?

"I'm sorry for being such a shitty brother. I knew you were doing the best you could. Just don't fucking leave us, man. You're the rock for us all. You can't leave us."

Brock.

Why would I leave? I own this fucking town. Brock, why would I leave? Again, his voice fades, and I'm stuck in silence. I don't know whether it's been seconds or days by the time the muffled sounds bring me to.

"I always knew Eric wasn't my father, but not a day went by I didn't consider you my brother. We still have the same blood running through us. I'm so fucking sorry. I'm sorry for not being normal. For being so wrong in the head. I just

couldn't see you bear a mistake I made. I don't regret what I did. And that's what's so fucking wrong with me. I would do it all over if given the chance. But this, I would never ask for this. If you die, I won't last. I need you. I need you to remind me I'm going to be okay. And I will tell you that you don't have to bear the burden of us all. We're together. All four of us. We're Pearsons. We don't let one another fall. So fucking wake up. Tell me it's going to be okay. Because if you die. It won't be, and I don't know what happens from there."

Why does Nixon sound so sad? I'm right here, brother. Don't feel the burden of me. I'm the one who holds us all together. I'm not going anywhere. I have an empire to run. A girl to marry. A brotherhood. Why is everyone so fucking sad?

The sounds of beeping get louder. I wish they would shut the fuck up, because I can no longer hear Nixon. I yell his name, but he doesn't respond. The beeping becomes louder, and then it's too many voices I hear.

"I need a doctor!"

"What the fuck is happening?"

"We need a crash cart! Code blue!"

"Hayden, NO!"

———

It feels different now.

No more sounds or voices.

Am I dead?

I can see color. I wasn't able to before. Fuck, I think I'm dead.

No! This isn't what I want. I need to go back.

"You look like a lost kitten. I thought I raised you better than that."

I turn, a figure appearing before me. "Dad?" Oh, fuck. "Am I dead?"

"Well, I hope fucking not. I didn't get my head shot off and leave my legacy just to have you follow me."

"Then how are you here? Where am I?"

"You're in a place where weak people go. People who don't fight hard enough for what they want."

I find that funny. "Says the man who got his head blown off for our underage neighbor."

"Who knew that asshole would turn out to be a motherfuckin' psychopath. I guess no surprise there. He sure got me there. Maybe the dollhouse should have clued me in. But my seed made its mark. He'll never get rid of me. So, in the end, I fucking won. Checkmate. Even though, it seems he didn't make it much longer on that earth."

"Are you here to guide me to heaven or some shit?"

"Fuck no, son. I'm here to tell you to stop being a pussy. I raised you to be tough. You may think the way I handled you was bullshit but look at the man you are today. A strong Pearson. Don't prove me wrong. This isn't your time. Go back and fight. Take what's rightfully yours. Make me proud."

I feel strange.

Can I cry where I am?

My father looks young. Like he did when we were

kids. It makes me realize how much I miss him. I want to hug him, and tell him that, but he starts to disappear. "Wait. Don't go."

He doesn't seem to hear me.

"Dad!" I yell, but nothing comes out of my mouth.

The damn beeping sounds again. I scream for my father to come back, but the beeping is so loud.

And suddenly, I feel like a million-pound weight is shoved into my chest.

THIRTEEN

K A T I E

Four days later...

"You ever going to go home and get a good night's rest?"

I lift my head to see Nixon walking in holding two coffees. "Yeah, when we're taking him home."

We're on day four.

Hayden has been in and out. The first two days were the scariest days of all our lives.

He flatlined twice.

They were able to stabilize him, and we've been smooth sailing since. The doctor pulled him out of his induced coma yesterday, so now it's just a waiting game. They said his body will know when it's time and to be patient. I'll wait forever so long as it means he *will* wake up.

I take the coffee and bring it to my lips. "Thank you. The hospital coffee is shit."

"It's probably what's putting people *in* the hospital."

I turn back to Hayden. He looks better. His color is returning and he's not so swollen. They took him off the drip this morning.

"Any changes?" he asks, pulling a chair up to the other side of the bed.

"No. I swear he squeezed my hand back in the middle of the night, but when I flagged down a nurse, she said it's probably just muscle spasms."

Nixon nods, taking in his brother. Everyone's been here every day. Nixon the most. Officer Forbes has checked in, hoping to get a statement, but it's been a wasted trip.

"Speaking of taking care of ourselves, you eat anything lately? You're looking a bit slim these days."

He growls and takes a large sip of his coffee. "You sound like Rowan. I'm fucking eating. Erica feeds me those nasty cheddar puffs all day long."

I laugh. "I mean real food. You're doing no one any good by running yourself down."

"Look who's talking," he says. "Why don't you agree to leave this room and I'll agree to eat something and we head down to the—"

"*Katie...*"

We both jump.

My eyes whip to his.

"Hayden?"

Nixon is up and out of his chair, running out and yelling for a nurse.

"Oh god, you're awake!" Tears instantly build.

"Katie," he says again, grabbing at his throat.

"Shhh, don't talk. You've had a breathing tube in. They took it out, but you're gonna be sore." I stand and lean over him. His hand is trying to lift, but he's struggling.

"What? What is it?"

"Mine," he croaks.

I choke on my own sobs. "Yes, I'm yours. Always yours."

———

HAYDEN

TWO DAYS LATER...

"I'm fine. I don't need it," I growl at the nurse trying to drug me up. They put me fucking out and I need to be alert. Focused. I worry if I fall asleep, I won't wake up.

"Mr. Pearson, you were shot. The medication is only going to help you stay comfortable."

"Don't fucking care. Get that shit away from me."

"He giving you trouble again?" She's back, thank god. I get anxious whenever she leaves. Her smile is the only drug I need.

"He won't take the pain meds. I keep telling him trying to tough out a gunshot wound is not the definition of bravery."

Katie laughs, and I swear I feel better already. "Such a big, bad man." That's fucking right. Before she went to get coffee, I had her gather all my brothers. I needed to know what really happened. Nixon told me the story I had to tell the cops as soon as I was coherent enough to understand. It also meant Katie was left in the dark.

Nixon was short when explaining no one knew the truth. But it was time. No more secrets.

Just as Katie takes her seat next to my bed, the door opens, and everyone piles in, including Trevor. Once the door is shut, I waste no time getting to business.

"I want to know what happened. And I want to know everything." I don't remember getting shot. I remember walking into the cottage and trying to talk to Nixon. They went down, and then things went dark for me.

Everyone looks around on who should talk, when Nixon steps forward.

"The day I stormed out of Eric's house, I left. I took

Rowan and Erica home, and I did some digging of my own. I knew Eric had cameras all over the outside for security. Not knowing if they were still running, I went back later to find out they were. Seems he had them on motion detectors. They turn on whenever there's movement. Since we had been there, they'd been running. It allowed me to get Jameson's license plate, which later led me to his house."

I remember going to his place, and the recording.

"He seemed to be ready and waiting. But I didn't realize he was expecting you. He was just as surprised to see me as I was when he mentioned you. I knew you were going to try to do something dumb. So, I just did it first. I brought him to the cottage, knowing it was the last place anyone would suspect. No one really knew about the place. I was going to make my problem go away. But then you showed up."

"What happened to Jameson," I ask calmly. I can't have another death on my brother's hands.

"I took care of him," Trevor steps forward.

Shock hits me. "*You* killed him?"

"No. I told you, killing wasn't the answer. But we made sure he would never be blackmailing anyone again."

I'm confused. "Explain, now," I snap.

This time, it's Brock who speaks up. "We made sure to get rid of the video first and foremost. He had one copy hidden in the house and one on his phone. Both have been destroyed."

"Jesus, what did you do?"

A smile creeps up his face. He takes a quick glance at Nixon, then Cam, who wear matching smirks. "Well, we burnt his shack down. Easy too. It was old, and they concluded it was caused by bad wiring."

"Jesus," I sigh. What were they thinking? Arson is just as big of a felony. "And his phone? What did you do to be sure he won't go to the cops or try to exploit us?"

The three of them begin to laugh. "Let's just say Ethan has a buddie who's into some sick shit and was willing to help us out. For a small price, we did a little blackmailing of our own. If Jameson Vincent ever tries to return to Tampa, blackmail us, or even thinks about talking, a certain video with him, a horse, and a few dudes will surface. He was A-okay with taking the deal."

I can't do anything but shake my head. Then I join them in laughing. Fucking Pearsons. Everyone starts to settle, and Nixon grabs his phone from the table.

"Gonna let you get some rest. We'll see you when you get released tomorrow."

I reach out and grab his forearm. He stops and our eyes collide.

"We're together. All four of us. We're Pearsons."

There's recognition in his eyes. He doesn't hide the tear that falls. He nods, knowing we're all going to be okay.

"Now, you can all get the fuck out so I can see about some hospital sex."

EPILOGUE

H A Y D E N

T WO MONTHS LATER...

"CANNON BALL!" BROCK YELLS AND JUMPS INTO the pool, sending a wave of water toward Rowan and Erica. I laugh at Trevor, who looks murderous for waking up a sleeping Eva nuzzled in her carrier in the shade.

Taking another sip of my beer, my eyes lock on the sliding glass door Lucy and Katie disappeared through. Katie left the condo in a rush this morning, saying she had a quick errand to run. She's been acting weird all morning, and I'm worried it's something I've done.

It's been two months since I knocked on Death's door and told him to fuck off. The conversations I heard still sit heavy in my mind. Mainly the one with my father. To this day, I wonder if he was real or just a dream.

The day I was released, I made a promise to myself to make a lot of changes. Life didn't owe me anything, and after almost losing mine, I realized I had so much to live for. My brothers, Katie, to see through the legacy of my father's company. I vowed to shape the fuck up. Be more responsible at work. Be less of an asshole. Basically, ditch the lifelong chip on my shoulder.

I've come to terms with the responsibilities in my life. I'm more thankful for my support system. I'm not angry for the weight I hold of trying to keep our family together. I'm grateful for it. Despite how we all felt about our father and mother, they gave us each other. We'll always have one another. Even if some of us cannot agree at times.

The fact will always remain.

We are Pearsons.

I don't deserve her, but Katie stayed. I worried she

made her decision because of what happened. I won't deny I had a few bad days where I reverted to my old self. But this time, she did what she swore she wouldn't do the second time around and didn't allow me to push her away.

Being shot and near death does something to a person. The first couple weeks, a cloud of depression set in. I wanted to blame myself for everything. Be angry at how I let things get so out of hand. But Katie. God, my Katie was there by my side every step of the way. She knew how to handle me. And that she did. She shut down all my craziness. She talked to me. She held me at some low moments. And in the end, I came out stronger. *We* came out stronger.

The last thing I wanted was for her to stay for the wrong reasons.

She told me she was staying because fate doesn't come around three times.

I agreed.

"Everything okay?"

Breaking from my thoughts, I turn to my right and notice Trevor has taken up the lawn chair next to me. "Why you ask that?"

"A lot of changes here to come. Not to mention you've been staring at that door for the past twenty minutes."

I pull my eyes away and take another swig of my beer. "Nah, it's all good. It's time." And it is. I finally made a decision on the house. I'm signing it over to Nixon. He wants to have ours and the Wheeler house demolished, and something built here to replace it. I'm all for his decision. I couldn't imagine another family living in this house with all the memories—good and bad.

Would they know the darkness that lived here? Next door?

I want us all to move on. We all do. And it seems impossible with all the memories that reside within these walls. Nixon has a plan. One I stand behind. He's going to make it possible for us all to move on. Heal.

More splashing and yelling, this time from Nixon as he guards Erica.

"You two work your shit out?"

He's talking about Brock. He leaves tomorrow to head back to school.

Another swig. "Yeah. I can't force him to work at Four Fathers. Just don't want to see him fuck his life up." I'm tired of fighting with him. He's so stuck on rebelling against anything I say. He would make a great addition to the company, but he wants to blow me off. Non-stop arguments. I'm over it. It's time I accept him for who he is and let him find his own way.

Another glance at the door.

I can't shake this feeling. I don't think I did anything wrong, but when she left, she looked concerned.

She wouldn't leave me. She loves me.

"What do you think those women are up to?"

I slam the rest of my beer and drop the empty bottle.

"I'm about to find out." I get up and storm inside. I'm done running myself down worrying what's going on with her.

I don't see them right away, but I hear their whispered voices coming from the back bathroom. My feet hit the marble floor and I reach the bathroom door and throw it open. Two startled females jump and turn to me.

"Jesus, Hayden, you scared the shit out of us!" Katie yelps.

"What the fuck are you two up to?" I ask, angry. They look guilty. My eyes break away from Katie's to the item she's holding in her hands.

What the...?

"What—?"

"It's not what you think!" she squeals, just as I grab the object in her hand. "Hayden..."

I stare at it.

I'm not fucking dumb either. I know what two blue lines mean.

"Hay—"

"Don't fucking say anything more." I snatch her up into my arms and bring her tightly against my chest. So many emotions run through me, I struggle with the right words to say. She's pregnant. With my baby. We're gonna have a—

"Hayden," she says my name again.

I kiss the top of her head and pull her away and cup her face. "I love you. Don't worry. This may not have been our plan right now, but the thought of you carrying my child...fuck." I give her a quick kiss and pull her back to my chest. "I'm gonna love this baby just as much as I love you. We're gonna get married, I'm gonna buy us a big ass house. World's biggest play center. The works." My heart is filling. I can't believe it. She's—

"Hayden!"

"Yeah, baby?"

"The test is Lucy's."

What?

I pull away and catch her eyes shining with humor. "This isn't yours?"

"No." She shakes her head and smiles. "It's Lucy's. She's pregnant again." I pull my eyes away from her and look at Lucy. She smiles and shrugs.

I look back at Katie. God, her smile does things to me. "I thought it was yours," I say, brushing some loose hair behind her ears. "Can I get a moment alone with Katie?" I ask, never taking my eyes off my woman.

Lucy is already jumping into action. "Yep! Got it. I'm just gonna go eat some juicy burgers before I break the news to Trevor and he drags me home." She stops at Katie to give her a hug. Then she turns back to me. "I'll...uh, take that." She grabs the test I forgot I was still holding out of my grip. "And sorry for the mishap, Hay. No diaper duty for you just yet." Lucy chuckles and pats me on the shoulder before heading out the door.

Once the door shuts, Katie speaks. "You look almost disappointed it wasn't me," she says, as if maybe reading my mind.

"I am and I'm not. If you were pregnant, I'd be ecstatic as fuck. But this just means more time for us before we bring kids into this world." I lean down and kiss her. "Because we're just beginning. One day, you'll be my wife, have a shit ton of my kids, and forever be my rock. That's not up for discussion."

Instead of trying to fight me on my bossiness, she smiles. She knows. She belongs to me. But it's no different for her. She knows with all of her being she owns me.

"So, what you're saying is you have plans for us?"

I have so many plans for us, I don't know where to start. A lifetime of happiness is first on our list. After a long fucking time of denying it, I'm finally going to embrace it.

I vowed the day she officially took me back I would never let her down. And I plan on keeping that promise. Starting with the lust filling up in those beautiful eyes.

My girl.

Always ready for me.

I bring my hands down her sexy stomach and go straight to the spot I crave to be. My fingers disappear into heaven as a sweet moan falls from her lips.

"You have no idea."

———

LUCY

"Who's fucking like teenagers in the bathroom?" Ethan asks as he walks in holding a bottle of something that probably costs more than all my organs if I sold them on the black market.

"Hayden and Katie. They're making up," I answer, taking another large bite of my cheeseburger. This thing is about to give me an orgasm it's so good. Two slices of cheese and double the pickle and I'm in pure heaven.

"What were they fighting about?" Trevor asks from next to me.

I shrug, taking another full bite. "Pregnancy test

Katie was holding."

"Shit, she's pregnant?"

Another bite. "Nope, I am."

I go in for another orgasmic bite when my cheeseburger is smacked out of my hands.

"Hey! That was like the best burger ever made! It had double everything."

"Wanna repeat what you just said?" Trevor's eyes are wide. Probably matching my own as I stare at the poor burger slowly dying on the ground. How long does the five second rule truly last nowadays? "Luce..."

Oh, yeah. "Oh, yeah, it was mine. Totally pregnant. I told you I was ovulating that one time in the shower. You didn't listen."

Still staring at me.

He could at least offer me a new burger. I decide I'm not too worried about what's on the ground. People ate worse shit back in the ancient days. I bend over to pick up my burg—

"Whoa!" I squeal as Trevor tackles me and stands, carrying me in his arms. "Dude, I need to finish that! It's my civic duty! It's practically calling my name!" Man, pregnancy cravings waste no time to kick in.

"Red meat is bad for pregnancy," he grumbles and walks down the patio. "Nix, watch Eva for a bit, will ya? I have to have a private moment with my wife."

I start to giggle in his arms. "Why private? Will there be food there? Possibly cheeseburgers?" He takes his hand, and instead of smacking my butt, he gives it a hard squeeze. "Because I have to fuck my wife and thank her for making me, yet again, the happiest man alive."

ENJOYED THIS BOOK?
MEET THE OTHER SONS

Four Sons Series by bestselling authors

J.D. Hollyfield, Dani René,

K Webster, and Ker Dukey

Four genres.

Four bestselling authors.

Four different stories.

Four weeks.

One intense, sexy,

thrilling ride from beginning to end!

This series should be read in order to understand the plot.

A FOUR SONS STORY

Who's the daddy now?

NIXON

KER DUKEY

OTHER BOOKS IN THE
FOUR SONS SERIES

NIXON
BY KER DUKEY

I am a hothead, a wild card, and son to a murdered man.
I crave the things I can't have and don't want the things
I can.

Now, I'm left to pick up the pieces—stitch our family
back together with a damaged thread.
This isn't the life I envisioned. And to make matters
worse, the women in our lives are testing the strength of
our brotherhood.

My name is Hayden Pearson.

I am the eldest—a protective, but vindictive son.
People may think I'm too young to fill our father's shoes,
but it won't stop me from proving them all wrong.

This series should be read in order to understand the plot.

A FOUR SONS STORY

Why choose one when
you can have both?

BROCK

DANI RENÉ

OTHER BOOKS IN THE
FOUR SONS SERIES

BROCK
BY DANI RENÉ

I am strong, athletic, and son to a man I always wanted to be. I had made plans, thought I was on that path, and then a bullet stopped not just my father's heart, but mine too.

I've been living a life I'm not meant to.
I want more. I want to escape.
And I found someone who's given me a love I never thought possible.

My name is Brock Pearson.

I am a free spirit who found happiness in an unexpected place. People assume I'll be another heir to our empire, but my heart belongs elsewhere.

This series should be read in order to understand the plot.

A FOUR SONS STORY

A ring won't stop
the determined…

CAMDEN

K WEBSTER

OTHER BOOKS IN THE
FOUR SONS SERIES

CAMDEN
BY K WEBSTER

I am intelligent, unassuming,
and the son of two murdered parents.
I'm calculating, damaged, and seek revenge.

I'll do whatever it takes to further my agenda, even if it
means seducing my way into a bed I don't belong.
Anything to make the ones who've hurt me pay.

My name is Camden Pearson.

I am focused, fierce, and power-hungry.
The youngest of four brothers.
People assume I'm the baby, but I grew up a long time
ago.

*** *This series should be read in order to understand the plot.* ***

ACKNOWLEDGMENTS

First, and most importantly, I'd like to thank myself. It's not easy having to drink all the wine in the world and sit in front of a computer writing your heart out, drinking your liver off and crying like a buffoon because part of the job is being one with your characters. You truly are amazing and probably the prettiest person in all the land. Keep doing what you're doing.

Thanks to my husband who supports me, but also thinks I should spend less time on the computer and more time doing my own laundry.

Thanks to all my eyes and ears. Having a squad who has your back is the utmost important when creating a masterpiece. From betas, to proofers, to PA's to my dog, Jackson, who just got me when I didn't get myself, thank you. This success is not a solo mission. It comes with an entourage of awesome people who got my back. So, shout out to Amy Wiater, Gina Behrends, Jenny Hanson, Kristi Webster, and everyone else who helped make Hayden amazing. I appreciate you all!

Thank you to Monica at Word Nerd Editing for helping bring this story to where it needed to be.

Thank you to All By Design for creating my amazing cover. A cover is the first representation of a story and she nailed it.

Thank you to my awesome reader group, Club JD. All your constant support for what I do warms my heart. I appreciate all the time you take in helping my stories come to life within this community.

Thank you to Emilie and the team at InkSlinger for all your hard work in promoting this book!

And most importantly every single reader and blogger! THANK YOU for all that you do. For supporting me, reading my stories, spreading the word. It's because of you that I get to continue in this business. And for that I am forever grateful.

Cheers. This big glass of wine is for you.

ABOUT J.D. HOLLYFIELD

J.D. Hollyfield is a creative designer by day and superhero by night. When she's not cooking, event planning, or spending time with her family, she's relaxing with her nose stuck in a book. With her love for romance, and her head full of book boyfriends, she was inspired to test her creative abilities and bring her own stories to life. Living in the Midwest, she's currently at work on blowing the minds of readers, with the additions of her new books and series, along with her charm, humor and HEA's.

J.D. Hollyfield dabbles in all genres, from romantic comedy, contemporary romance, historical romance, paranormal romance, fantasy and erotica! Want to know more! Follow her on all platforms!

STALK LINKS

Twitter
https://twitter.com/jdhollyfield

Author Page
http://authorjdhollyfield.com/

Fan Page
http://www.facebook.com/authorjdhollyfield

Instagram
http://www.intsagram.com/authorjdhollyfield

Join Reader Group
http://bit.ly/1dGxSwl

Goodreads
http://bit.ly/1vpfOZE

Amazon
http://amzn.to/2g4iwJm

NEVER MISS UPDATES!
Sign up for J.D. Hollyfield's Newsletter!
SIGN UP!

https://bit.ly/1C3QMnV

OTHER BOOKS

Love Not Included Series

Life in a Rut, Love not Included

Life Next Door

My So Called Life

Life as We Know It

Standalones

Faking It

Love Broken

Sundays are for Hangovers

Paranormal/Fantasy

Sinful Instincts

Unlocking Adeline

#HotCom Series

Passing Peter Parker

Made in the USA
Columbia, SC
28 August 2018